SOMEWHERE IN THE DARK

By

Kola Adeniyi

 New Generation Publishing

For

Kunle Adeniyi

A brother, yet more than a brother...
A friend, yet more than a friend...
A priceless companion...
Strength in times of weakness...
(And those times were dreary and long)
Courage in times of despair
(And again, those times were dark and seemingly
endless)

PROLOGUE

Things have gone wrong. Chikodi Njoku had been dogged by the premonition for weeks. But he had not been able to take any concrete action because he had no means of substantiating anything. Only precautions. Now his fear had taken on flesh and blood and was hovering over him, a deadly gun in hand. Worse is that the fear used to be a very trusted associate. "It's expedient that I do this quickly," the fear said, "You see, I have to get to the other criminal partnering with you in this crooked business of yours before news about this moment get out at all."

Somehow Chikodi believed this, but could not say anything. He just blinked and held his hands in a protective posture in front of his face, sinking to his knees as he did so. For a brief moment the manner in which Chikodi met this personified fear flashed through his mind. They were seatmates on a flight from Lagos to China, each going for his own businesses. Then Chikodi had leaned towards this fear and asked, "So how does it feel to be a Nigerian?"

"Great," the fear had replied. "You see, the bad shape of things actually presents great business opportunities for those who have the eye to see. I mean those who are smart."

This reply had made Chikodi regard him for a moment. Then he had said, "Yes, you're right. But those who have the eye must also have the will." On that they had agreed. The flight had been an eye opener for both of them as they rubbed minds on the way forward for themselves through the dwindling fortunes of their country. Chikodi could not deny the fact that this fear had observed quite correctly that he lacked one thing; connection in the right political circles. The fear had offered to help. And the result had been the partnership just about to be ended with the bullet. Oh! Chikodi now recalls the entire prelude to the partnership and how it had prospered, weathering every storm. He had to do something to stop this from happening. It was just about time the business weathered the final storm and Nigeria would be his, no, theirs. No, something must be done.

ONE

Omuya had a humble beginning. His father was from the Igarra tribe, a tribe known across the country for yam cultivation, and in neighboring states for extraordinary strength for menial farming works. The neighboring states knew the Igarra people, or Gara as some called them, so well because in spite of their niche in yam cultivation, they were always in need of suitable farmland for their expertise. So they were given to relocation season after season, just like the nomadic Fulanis; only that in place of cattle, the Igarras moved with their big hoes. Omuya was a son of one of such people; a man who traversed the middle belt region of the country for decades before finally settling in Ondo town where rather than cultivate yam, he did menial work on other people's farms.

Young Omuya would always be brought along with his father. At least as from the age of six. He would be abandoned in a part of the farm to eke out his own living with his little strength. Then while working on a cocoa plantation one hot afternoon, a cobra attacked Omuya's father, engaging the man in a fierce battle. At the end the man killed the snake, but not without severe bites. The little boy had watched the battle from a safe distance. And when after the snake had died, the man himself had fallen, the boy had raised an alarm. Luckily, people returning from their day's work came to the rescue. They rushed the man to the town for medical attention. Unfortunately, there was no antidote for snake venom at the nearest hospital and the man had to be rushed to another hospital in a neighboring town. No better luck. At the third hospital, they were told the bitter truth: the only place the antidote could be bought was the University College Hospital situated hundreds of miles away. Getting it was thus out of the question. So, the man had died right in Omuya's hands. With no means of giving his late father a burial at all, the boy had left the remains at the hospital veranda and fled. Whatever became of the body he never knew.

All that he knew was that his father would not have died if medicine had worked. He was going to be a life saver, if he had a way.

The boy had returned to what he had been taught, working hard at it. With no relation around and no idea of where home was, and no intention to return there anyway, the boy had sent himself to primary school, owing the school authorities almost all the fees throughout. In the secondary school, he had owed almost all the fees again. The teachers understood, so they did not even bother to ask him most of the time. But he had paid for his registration for the final exam. And he had passed. By a kind of intervention he had not been able to explain, he got a scholarship to study medicine.

But realities struck him after graduation. Doctors were not been paid a wage close to being commensurate with their input; they were not getting equipment to work with. They had no access to modern methods of their calling. Worse still; in spite of the fact that doctors engaged by the government were less than twenty percent of those needed to ensure health in the country, many had no jobs and those who had were being threatened with dismissal every day. And, of course, budgetary allocation to health was ending in national leaders' personal accounts. After hundreds of patients he could have saved had died in his hands, because, many times, of lack of common analgesic, Omuya had quit the profession out of frustration.

He had to do something that would bring money. With money, more lives could be saved than with the expertise of a hopelessly poor individual. Of course he could return later to marry his money with his expertise in saving lives. And just then he had met somebody who seemed to be willing to help him achieve his new dream.

***

Nsika Isaiah's father was a fisherman as was the way of the Niger-Delta people. The people believed that God had situated them in a place blessed with the abundance of water because he knew that they were going to get all they needed from water. And so they lived their lives. Even their security depended on water. At the sight of an enemy, an average Niger-Delta person could dive into the water and resurface after many days, and of course long after the enemy had gone. They could even fight all their battles from the water. But the greatest wealth their water had blessed mankind with had become the curse of the people. Oil, as it is called had been discovered in commercial quantity and they had been glad for the short time between the discovery and exploration, for along with the exploration came the pollution of their precious water, the source of everything to them. By the mid 1970s oil had become a major commodity in the World market with their country being a major producer. The misfortune for the region was that the more the oil produced the more the hardship dwellers of the region were subjected to. The explorers had ignored all their cries and had simply collaborated with the government to carry on as if no injustice was involved at ll. In the years that followed, the suffering of the people intensified so much that they had resorted to violence to press home their demands that they be treated like the custodians of this wealth.

But Nsika's father had not liked the violent

approach because rather than bring succor, it had brought about genocides and too many brutal killings. The man had been in support of superior argument for achieving the quest. "Patience," the old man had emphasized, "is the weapon." He had believed that in their patience the people of the region should send their children to school to get educated. With education, the man had argued, the battle would be more easily fought. In the line of his belief, he had sent Nsika to the university to study Law. "When you graduate," he had told the boy, "you'll join the people at the vanguard of the struggle against re-colonization by our next door neighbors long after the colonialists have gone."

But the boy had learnt in the university that selfishness is the way of the African man. And all he needed to do was see how he could explore the status quo to his benefit. He was going to take care of his own people afterwards.

Immediately following his graduation from Law School, Nsika had made a little professional noise about the state of the Niger-Delta people basically to be noticed by government; after that he had been invited to the government villa for talks. That was the point he got initiated into the cult of those who sought their own at the expense of the masses. Since then, he had not looked back.

Why should he?

***

Chikodi Njoku had always known that trading was his life. From the most ancient time history could probe into, the Igbo people had always been traders, going everywhere on the surface of the earth to carry out their enterprise. Even history showed that that was how they pioneered the coming of English to Nigeria. Igbo people would take any risk as long as they knew there was monetary gain on the horizon. But unlike the typical Igbo people, Chikodi's father had insisted on education for all his children. After education, he believed, anyone could go any direction they chose. By then, he would have done his bit as father. Thus the boy had gone to the university to study computer science. Unfortunately, Chikodi had admitted after graduation, he had not touched a computer throughout his studies in the university. Yet, he had done practical computer courses for the four year period. Well, one of the lecturers had always pointed out that what was being done was actually theory of practical. As bad as it was, the make-believe practical courses paid off, for Chikodi learnt that programmers stood the best chance of rising in the world of information technology in this part of the world where the capital for business start-ups was nonexistent. It was possible however for a programmer to create problems which he would later solve for huge amounts of money. Even beyond that, there was a somewhat brighter prospect; computer was just becoming known in his country and, with foresight, he knew that banks, manufacturers and many others would soon begin to scramble for it. The young man thought of establishing himself as a dealer. Then, he could plant a chip in every computer he sold. With those chips he would be able to access the data of the users of the computers especially the big companies and extract the pieces of information he needed. He was certain that his chips would grow to become money trees.

But still, he needed money to start this sure business. That took him back to the beginning. Only that now, he had a purpose; a sure one.

***

Chikodi Njoku, computer expert, Nsika Isaiah, Lawyer, and Omuya Ibrahim, medical doctor set out in partnership with the intent of drawing from the expertise of each individual for the good of all. Within them the business, which they were determined to grow to the class of fortune 500 companies, was known as The Trio Group, TTG. But it was never registered as the Trio Group, or as TTG; the name only existed on their mind. It was hardly mentioned, not even during their meetings. The group was not even registered at all. This was Chikodi's idea: they were to operate anonymously to avoid undue attention such as tax and envy. They were going to establish in different sectors of the economy under different names, one or two of them serving only on the board. But they were going to choose the people manning their businesses carefully to ensure loyalty. By this, they at a future time, when they had established themselves as a formidable force, would emerge from the blue to formally take dominion of the economy which they would have been controlling by proxy.

The first company they established was a computer software development company. The company developed financial management software for higher institutions and distributive trading companies. The software which was actually developed by an undergraduate who was with the company for industrial training, managed effectively large amounts of income and the numerous channels through which the incomes came. With little improvement, the software was adapted for banks and tax collecting agencies. The sentiment for indigenous products assisted in the push for its adoption by the federal government for its tax offices nationwide and government-owned specialized banks.

Then the Trio established in another name a

computer assembly plant. The plant then approached the federal government with the proposal to make personal computers available to every citizen in the bid to grow the country technologically. If the government would foot sixty per cent of the bill, the company was going to seek public and private operators to support. It was going to be the best thing to happen to the country, they assured government. In the background, the Trio made some contacts and the proposal sailed through, only with unwritten agreements that fifteen per cent of the proceeds would go to the accounts of certain government officials. It was a fair deal.

The Trio then ventured into the business of banking, first acquiring a moribund bank and turning it around in a very short period. The Trio subsequently pumped cash into the bank and grew it in leap and bounds; it rapidly became one of the leaders in the industry. But more significant was its positioning to cater to the drug barons. The banks assisted in the cleansing of their ill-gotten money and bringing it into the country as investment by Nigerian professionals in the Diaspora. The investment branch of the bank would then assist in finding suitable industries to invest the money. Most times however those industries getting the laundered monies were owned by the Trio.

For the Trio, this was a sure source of capital for business. And since the capital was usually long term in nature, they decided to venture into the real estate industry, building first a housing estate containing five thousand units in Lagos. This to them was a cash cow, since almost eighty percent of Nigerians were not adequately housed. And they knew that the helplessness of the government on the issue was to them an opportunity. The housing units were completed within two years, and then the government was invited to adopt it for its civil servants who, as they rightly claimed, were going to be grateful for it. With a word or two from the Trio on the side, the government agreed to make a down payment of forty per cent for the units while granting that the payment by the civil servants be deducted from source over a period of seven years. By the time it was two years the company had already made three hundred per cent profit on the estate.

Then the Trio floated yet another construction company to explore the opportunities hiding behind the bad roads across the country. The company which was floated in Germany and having German directors made a proposal to the government. They wanted to manage the country's road network in the North in what they termed a free service arrangement. But they were going to construct toll gates all over where they were going to raise just their capital back over time. The excess from the proceeds would be shared between the government and them in a ratio that appeared too good. Since they were not going to take anything from government and they were going to do this good work in the North, a region having ninety per cent of national leaders, the proposal was approved without fuss. The toll gates immediately became cash cows. Then the company proposed to extend their humanitarian service to the Western parts of the country.

But this time, the government was going to put down a larger part of the money. Since the project had succeeded in the North, the government conceded and footed the bill for the second phase of the project. Thus, the expatriate company began to make huge profit before commencement of operations.

By this time, the Trio had extended their hold on the banking industry by acquiring, using different names, six more banks. Three of the acquisitions were actually done by consortiums of foreign investors from Holland,

France and America. Nobody ever suspected that the foreign investors were actually the Trio, Nigerians living low-key lives in Lagos.

TWO

"The coming general elections," Chikodi was saying, "is going to be the best thing to happen to our empire." In the last general elections, the business guru, as Chikodi was fondly called by his associates, had talked his partners into supporting certain candidates for the sake of their business. He had argued that the idea was capable of opening doors to them when such candidates got into office. His theory had been accepted and it had been beautiful.

The first payback they got was on the policy regarding the importation of fairly used cars. Government had said that any car older than five years was not fit for Nigeria, but the favor had been that a company on whose board Chikodi served as an executive director was importing vehicles sometimes as old as fifteen years without check. In addition, the new cars the company was selling were being imported duty-free. Then even the importation of computers by his other company became duty-free. The argument had been that they were for the benefit of the country, as the nation had the vision of making all citizens own their personal computers within a short period. But duties had not been waived for the other importers; so they became unable to compete in the market. They were crowded out after a few months of huge losses. Those who had the fighting spirit resorted to smuggling; which still did not match up. Now by his prescience, Chikodi was seeing even better deals in their tactical involvement in the elections ahead. Actually their only role would be to fund the campaign massively enough to make the politicians indebted to them by the time they got into office.

Nsika understood. "Yes, you're right. But the stakes

are higher this time; we have to play it right, or we may be the losers for it, don't you think?" he directed the question to Omuya in his bid for approval.

But Chikodi did not give the other person space to make his contribution. He said, "The picture is clear actually. We can't miss anything. Of course we know that it's really not the popularity or even integrity of the candidates that count; it's the question of whether they belong to the party that controls the electoral commission, whether they are violent enough, whether they have enough money to share out."

"And whether your party is in position to influence the judiciary when the petitions start coming with convincing evidence," Nsika added.

"Yes. And these still describe our candidates well." Chikodi said this triumphantly. "You see, you should know by now that we're a group of geniuses. We can't get things like this wrong. We're already beyond that."

"Fine; that's great compliment from you. But still, let's not forget that even the party has not made its choice. And we know that funny things can still happen at any time. Choosing certain people can distabilise the party; people are desperate about contesting under the umbrella of this party. I believe we still need a little patience."

"What are you getting at?"

"I mean we should still lie low until the candidates emerge. The party leaders tend to think with their stomachs these days. They can decide to change anything should an unknown candidate approach them with superior promises of personal aggrandizement."

"Well you're right; only that if we wait till then, it may be too late. Or I should say that it will be too late. We need to know that we're not the only one playing this game. And by the way, what if we begin our support from providing what to give to the party leaders? We're only known to our man anyway. And even at that, whoever our man is knows only a fraction of us and what we're capable of doing. At the sight of any eventuality, we lose nothing but money. And we know we'd not have lost at all anyway. In this party, no candidate loses. You lose at the primaries; they make you a minister, or an ambassador or something big. We can't lose. It's not possible."

Nsika reluctantly concurred with this line of reasoning. "Well, I agree... but... anyway."

With that they reached a consensus on the way things would go in the election months, and Omuya, the third leg of the tripod, simply gave his silent consent.

But there were more urgent issues: the restiveness in the Niger Delta and the recapitalization going on in the banking industry. Chikodi had always believed that the recapitalization was bad news. To him, it was an ill-conceived idea that was bound to have disastrous repercussions. The group had gained control of seven of the banks in operation; but now the central bank was saying that the number of banks in the country would have to be reduced to about a quarter, stronger ones. And the governor of the Central Bank meant it. The problem now was not even the money; it's that the new ownership structure was likely to weaken their hold on their banks.

Too bad.

Nsika was saying, "I think we should just think of how to shore up the capital base of the banks first. 32 billion naira is not small money. And in seven places? Men, we have a big issue to deal with here." He quickly added before yielding the floor to somebody else, "And we know we can't bring in money from the other investments; it will be a backward flow. That's against our policy." Of course the policy in question was an unwritten one.

But Chikodi was seeing things differently. "Omuya suggested something to me yesterday. If the banks are going to come down to about 20, we may not need more than just 2 to do our business."

"Okay," Nsika said thoughtfully. "And the central bank is already urging banks to consider the option of merger and acquisition. Is that what you're seeing?"

"Of course, that's the easy way out of this."

"I see. So we do it like three here, four there?"

"Maybe not. I should say this is also Omuya's idea. The strongest can boast of 37 billion, if we add deposits, on paper. We may also need to do some other paper works. But it can have that much in capital. That is enough for it to survive, and even acquire one or two vulnerable ones towards when the deadline comes into view. At that time they would not have much leverage. Come join us or perish. As for the other six; we merge them. I gather that that would give the one to emerge about 23 billion, which could easily be made to look like its 35 anyway... with paper works that cannot be detected. Or we leave it at that and go to the capital market to do a public offer. All we need to get 9 billion will be mouth watering promises. Again, we will have no problem here; if others are already making those promises, why not us? And if at the end of the whole consolidation they deliver, we will. And if they don't, we may not, too. But it's going to be a general industry matter. With only about 20 banks, there is little government can do about it. They will only help."

"You, or Omuya, must be crazy." Nsika was smiling broadly. "But you see, when the help thing comes, if it comes to that, I hope people won't go to prison?"

Obviously Chikodi had thought this out and was prepared. "We're not bank CEOs and are not planning to be. We don't even need to be directors. Clean we are!"

"But if the bank directors are fired hard enough, won't they begin to confess to the truth of their papers and, you know, possible bad debts."

Chikodi was also prepared for this. "They will certainly have more to lose than us. They will have everything to lose actually. And remember that they will have the foreign proxies to deal with before getting to us. Our investments are done through corporations and Holding Companies. Our involvement is never direct and we can't lose our money. That's the truth. And even if it comes to it, we'll be shielded by our friends in power at any time. That's why we're funding their political ambitions. Besides, since we're able to see into the future, we shall have to choose carefully and ensure that the directors to emerge are the loyal ones."

"So?" This was said with a tone of agreement. And with that they mapped out how to move, and went on to other issues.

Developments at the Niger Delta were already threatening their interests in several oil companies. One of the oil companies had already been forced to close shop. And their refinery in Kenya had not been getting enough crude oil to work with due to the unrest. This translated to the refinery tending towards running at a loss. But to discuss this issue, Chikodi suggested that they wait for Omuya who had excused himself to use the bathroom. The doctor had been purging and had not really been a part of the meeting because of the frequency at which he had been emptying his bowel. But he had the reputation for dealing with issues with the precision of a surgeon. Obviously the medical side of the man was still serving him. And at the moment the group was in need of that residual ability of his.

***

Since his last romance with death, Joseph Meals had decided to be a little more of a family man. The prompting was his realization that an African who dies without a child is said to have perished. Besides, his being unmarried at his age is also seen as a sign of irresponsibility by the culture. Marriage always brings responsibility; and managing it makes the man less restless, less daring and more determined to live. So he had taken Joyce to the court in the company of his siblings and her friends as witnesses. Her father had been incarcerated, and for that reason, a wedding with the usual African pomp had been ruled out. All they had done was get the man's consent, which, surprisingly, he gave without fuss. Now, his wife was pregnant and the pregnancy was with serious health challenges.

Joe had been sad when his family doctor had pronounced that she might have to be remanded to the bed throughout the pregnancy period. He only thanked God that after 6 months, she had been able to move around the house and do some house chores. She now also went to the church once in a while. Well, that was no surprise, for the time of her bed rest was a time spent studying the Bible. She even told him one evening that she had given her life to Christ. Who preached to you and how did it happen, was his response. But her account of a preacher in the dream and subsequent conviction through the Bible which had left her with no other choice than running to Christ was not so convincing to Joe. What she never said however was that the safety of her husband was a fear that had driven her to Jesus.

She could not bear to lose her husband after what had happened to her father. She even told Christ about it. Could you please save my dad, Lord? She had requested.

Joyce had not grown up with her mother. When she was still a toddler, the story went, her father, then a soldier, had returned from a peace keeping mission, only for his wife to abandon the girl and elope with a Europe-based rich man. That had lead the man to adopting the doctrine that says money is everything to a woman. The man had told her further that he had retired from the Army to become a nursing father, taking care of her. But all that had been uneventful until the last two years.

The man had been the chief security officer to the late president of the country, and had been loyal to him. He had been able to provide for all Joyce's needs at school. Suddenly her father had killed the president in cold blood, and had willingly given himself up for arrest. In his confession to her just before the murder of the president and the letter that the man had left for her afterwards, he had apologized earnestly, saying that he had not known the details of the atrocities of the president until he had got to a point of no return. He had gone ahead anyway and had done what was beyond pardon. He had decided to kill the president because he, the president had had the capacity to pervert justice and would have done just that, while the executor of his agenda would go down at that point in time.

The whole episode had played to the advantage of Joseph Meals, the reporter whose quest had thrown open a terrible can of worms. Coincidentally Joyce had been his fiancée, and her father would have killed him. But she happened to have been the person at the reporter's house at the time. Thus, the old soldier had found himself at the verge of killing his only daughter. That was when the man had broken down and had made the confession, and had killed the president and had written an apology letter to her and had been whisked off to prison.

Two years ago.

With the nature of the man's offence Joyce did not really believe that he could be forgiven. But for Jesus to have prayed a prayer of forgiveness for those who crucified him, perhaps, God could still have mercy.

So, with little faith in what she was doing, Joyce still prayed for her father regularly.

She looked into Joe's eyes and said, "Honey I want to ask you something."

"Go ahead, my dear; I'm all ears."

"It's…its sort of odd that we've not mentioned it all these years, but…I don't know," her voice deliberately trailed off.

"So let's talk about something odd then. Say it," Joe urged, putting aside the newspaper he was reading.

"Are you sure?"

"Why not, you're my wife? And in any case I don't know what the subject is yet. But I think the earlier you say it, the better."

"Okay," Joyce said as if it was just then that she made up her mind to discuss the subject. "You're an African man;" she saw in the period of her brief pause that Joseph nodded, "how did you come by the name 'Meals'?"

Joseph found himself struggling to suppress a laugh to avoid embarrassing his wife. He could not help smiling broadly anyway. "Now I know why you said it's odd," he said, sitting up. "But is it?" he asked rhetorically, opening wide his arms. "Our people are given to adopting foreign names these days. Even traditional rulers bear John, Jonathan and all that. Do you think there is a big deal about that?"

"I hope you're not trying to parry my question?"

"Am I?"

"I think you're trying to. Because Meals is not in the same class with Peter, Johnson or whatever you call it."

"But Meals makes sense, doesn't it?" he pulled her leg.

"That's not what I'm talking about. Your ancestors certainly didn't bear Meals," she snapped.

"I hope you're not getting angry?"

"What if I am?"

"If you get angry because I'm playing with you, I won't like it."

"So stop teasing me and tell me what I want to hear. It's a serious matter to me."

"I don't like your tone. And you know you get upset easily these days." Joseph was smiling all the same.

Joyce realized that this was true. The pregnancy had pushed her to her wit's end. She relaxed in her seat, turned slightly so that she now was not looking directly at him anymore. "I'm sorry," she said slowly. Then she faced him again, "So, will you now tell me?"

"Thank you for saying you're sorry. It's one of the reasons I love you so much."

"So?"

"Give me a piece of meat from your pot and I'll tell you what you want to know."

"Of course you know I will." Joyce went into the kitchen and returned with a plate full of meat.

"Woman, do you want to kill me with cholesterol?"

"Just eat what you want and I'd return the remaining."

"You won't give up; will you?" He did not wait for an answer. "So, sit down and I'll tell you what my father told me." She sat and Joe made a big show of eating a piece of meat. Then he said, "My dad was the first to enroll at the school sited at our village. So people said he rushed there because he knew the white men were going to give food to students."

Joyce was looking at him.

"'Food, you'd agree with me, has a semantic link

with 'Meal'. And my father was said to have always been happy at meal time. So friends nicknamed him 'Meals'."

"That was an alias." Joyce did not appear satisfied.

"Yes it was. But he was never apologetic about anything he did. And to prove that, he accepted the nickname proudly. Teachers soon joined in the name-calling affair, and from there, it sort of became formal. Interestingly his own father's name was Agbetuyi, the name itself having a lot to do with food. So if you call Meals a mischievous translation of Agbetuyi, you'd actually be right." Joseph stopped talking for several minutes; he just looked intently into Joyce's eyes. Then he added, "So...here we are. Do you want us to change back to Agbetuyi?"

"Oh, no. Is that the whole story?"

"Yes, that is the summary, and I think it is even generously comprehensive."

"It's interesting," she smiled, "Meals!" She now adjusted in her seat so that she sat next to him, brushing her shoulder against his. "So why were you dodging the question?"

"I wasn't dodging it. I was interviewing you."

"How?"

"You wanted to join me in the reporting business, didn't you?" Joyce nodded. "But you've got to learn patience, persistence and a lot of tolerance. Many times, all you need from the people you interview is not more than a line, but they will play you for a long time. You get angry, and you lose it. You lose concentration; you won't know when the line has mistakenly slipped out of their mouth. You see, you failed the interview on many fronts."

"Therefore?"

"There is no vacancy at my publishing house. Go and practice Law and you'd have many justification for being angry with the government. I'm sorry, but I believe you'll excel at law, not at journalism…or far better than journalism. And you know; my chamber is still there. I will not have to recommend you, just walk in and introduce yourself as Mrs. Meals. That's all."

"Don't try that with me," Joyce snapped, pulling away from him.

But Joseph replied as calmly as he could, "Journalism is too dangerous for you, my dear. Too many people have things they want to hide at all cost, and that to the detriment of the masses. I can't allow you get involved there."

"Rather, I'd say that you made it dangerous for yourself. I'll do stories on health, HIV and the emancipation of womanhood. I have yet to see the danger in those areas."

"There you go again. The company of women who dare their husbands; my people call it the club of 'what will the husband do?'"

"No, no, no, I'm not a feminist. And you know that," Joyce snapped again.

"Now you're angry again. I told you you're not qualified for journalism."

Joyce could not respond to that because just then Joe's phone rang. It was Nura Taiwo, the estranged chairman of the ruling political party.

With the way Nura Taiwo spoke, Joe knew that his fragile peace was about to be punctured again. The man wanted to see him urgently. He was even offering to come down to his house. "I'm humbled sir. But I'm too small to have you under my roof. I'll be at your place first thing in the morning."

"Good. I'd be waiting. My regards to your wife."

Now, Joe was certain, life was going to get perilous yet again.

Joe got to Nura's house at seven in the morning. He

was surprised that the gate opened just as he approached it. He drove into the compound and found no gate man around. Then the gate closed by itself. He drove all the way to the entrance of the house anyway and parked just beside Nura's car. It was then that he realized that the gate had been remote-controlled, and the opening had been done by the big man himself. Even at that early hour, he was fully dressed and was waiting at the door.

"Good that you're able to make it my compatriot."

"Thank you sir." Joe stepped out of his car and approached the man. "But I thought I was going to meet you still in bed. Is this not too early for your age?"

"What is that?"

"I mean you were up too early, for an old man like you. When do you really rest?"

"But I'm not an old man yet." They shook hands and went into the house.

Hot tea was waiting at the table and they went straight to it. After a sip, Nura said, "Let me not keep you guessing for too long. I know you're a busy citizen. There's this thing going on that you may be interested in." Joe had dropped his mug and was paying attention to the elderly man. "Some business men may have colonized the country economically, through corporations registered in different names. It will be difficult to trace any of the companies to them. But I'm positive that they own those companies. They have dominated every sector of the economy, and they are waxing stronger everyday by breaking rules with impunity."

The man looked at the reporter. "Would you be interested in a matter like that?" Of course he already knew what he had said was enough to make the issue irresistible to Joe.

Joe merely nodded. "I won't be able to tell until you

27

tell me who these men are."

Nura found that a blow below the belt, for he knew exactly what the reporter was referring to by the statement. "These should not put you in that kind of danger. Like I said, they are individuals like everybody. So you can choose to investigate them or investigate the companies. I have a list. At the end of the day, it's the link that matters. And we need to know how their operations are being done." Nura paused to lay open the piece of paper. Then he said, "Who are they?" He went ahead to mentioned a few names.

Joe was not sure whether he could believe this. But he did not say so. He promised the elderly man to look into it soon, and let him know what his line would be. The man gave him a list of just about five names.

As he drove through the gate, Joe knew he was back in trouble. This may look doubtful at the moment, but the position of the man in the society suggested that he knew what he was talking about. Just then the peril of two years ago, the one that had left Joe traumatized for months, came to mind….This same Nura Taiwo, though anonymous at that time, had requested him to investigate the link between a public figure and a series of crimes buried in the past. He had given him some clues and equipment, and even a car, saying they were to aid his work. Joe had not considered the risk before proceeding on the investigation. As it turned out, he had almost got killed; his fiancé had actually come face-to-face with death; and his brother-in-law had actually got killed in the process. As it happened the crimes were real and the big man was the president, who was determined to wipe out every trace of the crimes, especially human traces. In the process also, Joe had watched people killed, but had become a hero.

Deep within him however, he had regretted quitting his successful practice of law for journalism. He had feared that from then on, his life was no longer safe, as people who had secrets would mark him as dangerous and would want him out by all means because they knew they would not know about his moves until it had become public.

For those reasons Joe had relaxed a bit and expended his attention and energy on his family. And now that he was just getting over the unpleasant episodes, the same man had popped into his life again with another keg of gunpowder.

But he was going to exercise caution this time. And Joyce, oh, this woman needed him now more than ever before. And this idea, or the kind of attitude he demonstrated during those perilous times must not be repeated at this time. He was now married. He now had serious family commitments.

Joe knew the right thing to do: call the man and tell him he was sorry. But he could not bring himself to doing it.

He would summon the courage later.

THREE

Gabriel still remembered it all. He remembered when, why and how his father died at the prime of his years. Yes. Several decades after that gruesome event, he still remembered so vividly how his father's tongue was removed and his intestine sliced all because he dared to be at the vanguard of the crusade for the liberation of the Niger Delta. Gabriel remembered that his father died for the same course he had chosen today. He still very much remembered his father's last sentence: "Son, nothing can be as gratifying as committing oneself to the freedom and well-being of the people he love; in life and in death." The poor man paid the supreme price.

Gabriel looked up, at the people around him, partners in the crusade, and began to speak slowly, but emotionally. "As far as posterity has in record, this is our land, our heritage, our lifeline. And equally as far as same knows, the blessing of our heritage has been the cause of our woe, causing carnage, massacre, cold-blooded murders, maiming and the likes, all put together, getting too close to genocide lately.

"And we do not know what tomorrow will bring. Only that we will rather die fighting for our right and freedom than be subjected to the gradual humiliating death of oppression.

"We will stand up and fight. We shall be free. By God's grace. And I do not have more to say today than charge you to remain absolutely undeterred, resolute, and optimistic. We shall win.

"Nobody, I repeat, nobody shall succeed in stealing our heart, nor our heritage. No way. We shall win. Oppression shall pass. Mourning shall pass. The practice of hiding in your own land shall pass someday.

Joy is just around the corner, so close, so beautiful. I can see it! Stretch, my people, stretch. And stretch even more. Soon, we shall grab it, and rejoice that the blood of the thousands that have died kept us going, and fighting…and brought the victory at last. We shall win." To conclude, he repeated, this time forcefully, "We shall win!"

For several minutes after Gabriel had stopped speaking, Jude, the host of the group kept looking at him, beyond the rough skin and deep sad eyes through to the passion burning inside him. Indeed, Jude reasoned, Gabriel was a person who held firmly to the last line of the group's anthem. *And when all else fails, let the passion for freedom burn even the more.*

Jude himself had been a vibrant leader of this group, when he was a youth, when he was poor; when he had not collided with the powers that be, the very sect well above the law, and right at the foundation of all these trouble. "I want to salute your courage," he began. "And I want to let you know that for this course you have determined to fight, both the rich and the poor, the old and the young, the strong and the weak," he paused, out of inexpressible regret, "the living and the dead are strongly behind you. The spirit of our ancestors will see you through.

"Keep the spirit high, keep the fight going; we're almost there. And that's why I've agreed to host you at this time; to give you all the support I can… financially… and of course materially. There was an eruption of applause and he kept quiet to allow calm return to the room.

When calm eventually returned, Jude brought out a briefcase from under his desk and handed it over to Gabriel. Gabriel stood and took it from him. "In there," he said, "is two point five million naira cash." Another loud applause erupted. It lasted for ten minutes.

"Finally comrades," he shouted to gain the attention of his hysteric audience. When he did, he continued, "There are two jeeps parked outside now. And in each are fifty rifles and other necessary weapons to the struggle. Be careful. And remember to call whenever you need help. Thank you all, and God help you."

There was another eruption of applause, which after fifteen minutes, transited into the recitation of the group's anthem.

The land is ours
The fortune is ours
But all was stolen
Before our very eyes

Now the water is poisoned by oil spillage
The land has become death knell
And the air is polluted
Yet we're deprived
Of what belongs to us
Of our source of alleviation
Of our own fortune
By our so-called brothers

But our soul is not polluted
And because of that
We shall take back our fortune
We shall lay down our lives
Yes
We shall lay down our lives
We shall fight the course
We shall always remember
The saying of our ancestors

"And when all else fails, let the passion for freedom burn even the more."

While the anthem was going on, members of the group were touching knuckles with Jude one after the other and exiting the house. The last line was sung as Gabriel's knuckle touched Jude's. They held it together for a little while; then Gabriel let go and hurried after his compatriots without a word.

*　*　*

The two Toyota jeeps navigated through muddy roads with ease. Gabriel was behind the wheel of the one in front and his next-in-command behind the wheel of the other. All the people in the jeeps were members of the Movement for the Liberation of the Niger-Delta, MLND. The jeeps negotiated a sharp bend and were now on a highway. Riding on roads like this in this part of Nigeria had always been saddening to Gabriel. The fortune 500 oil companies had ignored the whole neighborhood and made for themselves highways connecting their residences, oil wells and office complexes only. Were they blind? Or didn't they see that the whole area was in need of motorable roads? And to worsen the situation they were showing the few roads over and over again on the television to prove that they are providing roads and other amenities for the local people.

Well, Gabriel thought, they are in for a surprise. He braked sharply and brought the jeep to a stop. The other parked just beside his. There they blocked the road and each of them hoisted his rifle as they hid in the bush by the roadside.

In less than five minutes, a Rolls Royce cruised by, honking as it approached. Another injustice, Gabriel thought in his hiding place; magnifying the gap between the wealthy foreigners and the poor locals by flamboyant lifestyles. A uniformed man alighted from the front passenger seat and approached the Jeeps. They realized too late that it was an ambush. The driver thought better of his attempt at a u-turn when he saw that the pointing guns were too close to his head.

"Can you please come down?" Gabriel requested of the executives sitting at the back. When he saw that they hesitated, he added, "If you love your lives more than your company, that is." They understood the threat and alighted immediately. Gabriel then ordered, "And your hands up in the air."

"What's going on here?" one of them managed to demand.

"You'll soon find out." A gun made contact with the skin of the neck of the one who spoke. Then he understood.

A letter was given to the driver of the car before he was released.

After they had settled in the Jeep, Gabriel said to the executives, "You really don't need to panic. We only want to feel your aristocratic presence in our local place. By that, we also believe you'd know firsthand what the local people are going through; and what they actually need. I hope you understand me?" he looked directly into the eyes of the one sitting beside him. "Then you'll shake off whatever we ask in ransom and go out there to do what is right, right?"

"You mean you're kidnapping us?"

"I don't think so. But you're free to call it whatever you want. We know we're only inviting you to keep us company, as well as asking for our due. That's all."

"But that's not right, and you know that."

"Actually it isn't. But you see, we employed the right approaches for decades, and yet we're not heard, seen or cared for. Now we've run out of them. And don't you try to lecture me on what is right; reserve your judgment for your employers. They will very much need it, especially after you've lived with us for a week."

"No, no, no, you don't have to do it that way. Just mention what you want and as soon as we return from the oversee meeting we're going for, we'll talk and do something to help you people."

"I see you're naïve, or still playing games with me. But I'll tell you this: we want more than anything in the world that you live with us in the riverine ghetto for a week and learn what no book can teach you on the subject of equity." Gabriel's mood changed abruptly and he said, "Look Mr. Director, would you just stop talking and allow me to concentrate on my driving?"

***

The Rolls parked in front of an expansive building. The driver got out and sprinted up the stairs immediately. He made for the office of the highest-ranking person available. He budged into the office without warning and thus met him in a provocative position with his secretary. "I'm sorry sir," he said. "I have a letter for you."

"Is it your duty to dispatch letters?" the man queried angrily. "You're a driver, so get out of my office now!" He pointed to the door.

But the driver was shivering. "Sir, the MD, armed robbers."

"What do you mean? Get out!"

"They took him away sir. In the black Jeeps."

"Who? Were you not the one who drove him to the airport? What are you talking?" the man was beginning to calm down as the Secretary's buttons were now properly done. He now saw that he had not taken the letter from the driver. He took it, tore it open and began to read.

35

***

In spite of the effort of the company and the police to keep the kidnap away from the public, at least, until concrete facts with which to face the press were got, news of the MD's abduction got out. Now the police division in charge of the area was under siege. Myriads of questions were flung at the Divisional Police Officer. And he had no answers whatsoever. Well aware of how the press was taking the matter, he did not know whether to own up and say he had nothing, not even a hypothesis…He delegated an Inspector to attend to them. "Just dismiss them," he instructed. "Tell them I'm out working hard to bring the culprits to book. For now we really can't comment on the issue. They should keep their ears to the ground; maybe they can even get information that is helpful. We'll have a news conference soon. That's when we're going to brief them on it."

The officer left and returned thirty minutes later. "Sir, they insisted that I speak to them for the sake of the public who were still in the dark. And some of them were afraid that more people might be kidnapped, that the public should be alerted."

"And what did you say?"

"I told them there is no need for that now. There is no indication that it will go that way.

"Good. I…"

"But they were not convinced. They asked for the exact time of the press conference, claiming that some of them had travelled in from Lagos and would not return until there was something to go back with."

"So what did you tell them?"

"I told them within the next 48 hours."

"You what!" The DPO shot up from his swivel chair, his bulging stomach brushing against his desk in the process. He banged his fist on the desk many times and finally clenched his fist. "Two days?"

"Sorry sir. They were wolves."

"Shut up! Do you know what you've done? We don't have men to run around; we don't have a telephone, and we don't have the vehicle to work with and you've made a promise already?"

"Sorry sir."

"Sorry for yourself. Now go and fuel the motorcycle. You'll go and speak with some boys."

"Its two tires are flat sir."

"Fix them."

"The exhaust is leaking sir."

"Fix it. Or go and buy another one. And be very fast because you have just about forty-five minutes to report back at the office. Do we have weapons on deck?"

"The AK-47 available is bad."

"Take it like that. No pistol?"

"They've been taken on patrol."

"Just fix the bike first. And get a corporal to go with you."

"Yes sir."

***

At the oil company, executives who were normally around only biannually and for less than two hours each time had been sitting round a conference table for about five hours. They had been speechless most of the time, each man thinking his thought, formulating and falsifying own hypotheses simply because the kidnappers were still faceless, nameless and reachless. And waiting for the stipulated time could be frustrating, and even disastrous. To worsen the situation, the police appeared to be as helpless as the most untrained civilian. The last contact with them had indicated

37

clearly that even with their gun, training and weaponry, the police were merely gambling. Gambling with people's lives. And that, almost two days after the kidnap!

"I suspect," one of the executives began as if he was merely soliloquizing, "that the local boys are behind this."

"Really?" came the reply from the head of the table. "For two hours now, I've tried to figure out the 'why' and I've not seen one." The man looked to his left and to his right hand. "Anyone able to think of a likely motive?"

"Some months ago, they requested that we help the communities and we gave them the dollar equivalent of what they asked for, though up till now, the project is still yet to start."

"But we gave them the money all the same; that's it," another man came in. "And they know it. I don't think it's them." He threw his pen on the table. "And remember, they were reported to have crossed the road with two jeeps, one of which they used to take our men away. Local boys can't have that, can they?"

"For all we know," the man at the head of the table interrupted, "they're the only one we can figure to having a motive-valid or not- for now. And they could hijack cars. They're armed enough to do that, at least."

"I think that's a strong reason. Should we tell the police to explore it?" someone else offered.

"No!" Everyone looked sharply to the head of the table. Then the man explained, "I don't see the police solving this thing the way we will like. Lives are on the line and we can't afford to settle a conflict like this with the gun. I'd suggest we contact the men who represented the communities in our last negotiations. We have their phone numbers; don't we?"

"Only one of them. A man named Jude."

"Then let's call him."

One of them left the room to get the complimentary card of the negotiator. He met a cleaner at the door, but the cleaner was cleaning the floor. It did not occur to him that cleaners rarely cleaned floors at this part of the company toward the end of the working day. He returned with the card, but the cleaner was gone. He did not notice that too. He went straight into the board room, placed the telephone at the center of the table, put it on speaker, and began to dial.

The room became quiet.

The call was answered promptly. Before they could say anything, the man on the other end of the line dropped a shocker. "This must be Bright Moon Petroleum."

They were dumbfounded. But the man at the head of the table recovered soon enough. "Yes, you're right. Hello?"

"Good. My accuracy is not in question actually. Besides my wife and little daughter only you have this number. And none of those could call me now because they're right here with me. So, what can I do for you?"

Relieved, the man replied, "We have a small problem on our hands and we feel you might be of assistance, the area being your turf."

"Go ahead."

"Our MD was abducted two day ago," the man paused considerably to allow the fact sink, "by some youth in black Jeep. Right now, we're desperate for assistance from anyone."

"I hope you're not suggesting that those were my..."

"Oh, no, no, no. We're only asking for help."

"Well. Did you say black Jeep?"

"Oh yes."

"Where did it happen?" They gave him the location,

and he promised to ask around. Then he remembered something. "By the way, was he taken along with the car?"

"No. the driver and the car were left. But another management level staff was taken with him."

"Oh! No! I was thinking of tracing the car, and I was sure we would get them. But this. Do you have plate numbers?"

"The Jeeps didn't have, according to the report of the driver. But we believe they are new Jeeps. There were nylons on the seat and all that."

Again, the man said "Oh! No!", but he added, "Well, let me see what I can do. But the police are in the best position to help here; don't you think?"

"They're also working on it."

"That's good. I'll get back to you." He hung up.

Immediately after the call a cleaner stepped away from the window of the board room, and went to a corner within the premises of Bright Moon Petroleum where she pulled out a cell phone. She placed a call to Gabriel and conveyed everything that transpired to him with an amazing precision. As uncertain as she was about the identity of the man who promised on the phone to help, she was still able to say he had a very deep voice characteristic of shouting into the phone, had a wife and daughter, and probably lived with his family. Gabriel did not need more to figure out the rest. The oil company had taken the expected channel. He was in control.

Gabriel was behind the wheels of a Volkswagen Beetle when the call came in. As he hung up; he turned into a narrow street. He had got to the outskirt of the capital city. In the last two days the group had relocated four times, each taking them farther from the Niger Delta region where they started from. And they had changed vehicles six times.

As the Volkswagen pulled up in front of a lone house, a tattered Toyota van pulled up beside it. Gabriel and his envoy filed out of the two vehicles, their honored captives in their midst. They proceeded into the house, where an armed guard was waiting. The guard opened the door for all of them to enter, then entered after them, locked the door and pocketed the key. He then led them on.

There was no talking

They exited the house through a back door and crossed a light brush, two deserted streets and finally entered a brothel. As soon as they were in the brothel, the guard turned to Gabriel. "He wants to see only you and the visitors. Last room on the right."

Gabriel then led the captives into the room.

"Good! That's what you are! Good!" The man exploded as soon as he saw Gabriel. He gave him a firm handshake and a tight hug and a loud "good of you!"

As soon as they were seated, Gabriel introduced his hostages by name, but neither himself nor his host. Then he switched to their local language, one he was sure the captives did not understand, "What sort of location is this for God's sake?"

The host replied, in another local language, "For God's sake it's a nice little place I've got for myself in Nigeria. And I like it. You'd also fall in love with it after listening to this recorded news. He gave him a headset and switched on the radio cassette player. The news left Gabriel speechless for several minutes after the cassette player had been switched off.

Then the host said, in yet another language, "Now this is a place in the center of Nigeria where nobody can suspect. Hide from your enemies by staying too close to them. That's the logic. You're safe, my friend! Nobody can find you here. So, what are your plans?"

"Do you have a Telephone here?" One was handed to him and with it he accessed his voice mailbox to get abreast of things. The expected message was there. It was left by the man with the deep voice. And it said to call back as soon as Gabriel heard it. He called the man.

The man must have been waiting for the call, for he answered on the first ring. "Gab, where on earth have you been?"

"Here and there, as is the way of an activist," Gabriel spoke in a local language, clearly indicating to the man that English was forbidden at the moment.

"I suppose you still have the men."

"The guests from the oil company? Oh yes, I do."

"Then we have to meet straight away."

Gabriel seemed to consider this for a few seconds. "But there is a small problem. I'm so far from the Niger Delta I don't even know where I am. I only know that I'm in safe hands...touring."

"How do you mean?" The man with the deep voice was surprised. Since the beginning of the clamour for welfare by the Niger Delta people, no kidnapper has ever been taken out of the region for that was the area their security was most guaranteed...in the creeks. This was a dangerous departure from the norm, and especially bad for the interests the man represented.

"I mean I'm safe here. Don't worry about me. What about the men?"

"I'm interested in their case. Their company will do anything you ask. Just let them go at once, and come for negotiation. I'll be your advocate and ensure that you succeed. Trust me."

"But," Gabriel pointed out, "You've been in my shoes before and you know how heartless and dishonest these people can be. I..."

"Gab, you should understand that I've been suspected already, and it won't take too long to trace it

42

all to you. You know the implication to us...to the whole region. We can't afford an escalation. I hope you've heard of the talk of force by the government. They may not reach you, but they will certainly get to the old people in the villages, the children, the women, those who cannot help themselves. Try to understand. One of these men is American. Those people are ready to go all out to recover their own."

"I was actually thinking we should be announcing our involvement in these kidnaps now. They need to know that we're not afraid. We'd rather die than live in fear. They should know that if they talk hard they loose. And our loss can't be worse anyway. We're at the lowest ebb. He who is down needs not fear a fall. They won't do anything to our people. Let these ones live like us for some time. I promise to deliver them alive."

"Gab, you've already achieved your purpose. They can't object to your terms anymore. Talk to them now, I mean their headquarters. But they've already told me they were ready to pay up to five million naira ransom."

"We may have achieved it with the companies; not with the government. And as for the offer, tell them to spend two hundred percent of that on providing social amenities for the area. At least that will do for a start. Then maybe we can start our negotiation."

"No, Gab, let's make do with the offer. I'll talk them into the amenities thing and get to you soon. But I can't guarantee that they will spend that much. And you know it's not going to be instantly. You've got to take them for their word. And I know they won't play games."

As Gabriel heard the click terminating the call in the earpiece, he turned to face his guests, broad smile on his face. All the while he had ignored the men. But now he told them to take their seats. "You'll be alright," he assured them. "You'll be alright," he said again. Then his mood changed, the smile completely gone. "But we won't," he stated regretfully. "Until justice is achieved, we won't be alright in the Niger Delta."

The MD saw this as another opportunity to engage his captor in dialogue. He stifled a sneeze, "You'll be alright my brother."

"Mister Man you don't understand what I'm talking about. Do you drink the stream water from the Niger Delta? That's what we drink. The water that you pollute. We still drink it because we don't have any choice. How long can you stay without electricity? We don't have it at all. You have the resources to acquire all that you need in life. We are poor. We live in lack in the midst of plenty. How can you say we'd be alright when the government is not doing anything about it; when all you are interested in is exploitation?"

The MD was sorry. He did not know how to respond to the tirade. So he said nothing. He just shifted his attention to his shoes.

Five minutes later the man with the deep voice called back with the news of the agreement. He then pleaded with Gabriel to let the men go. This time, it was outright plea. So Gabriel knew that he could not but let his captives go. Gabriel and his men waited till night and drove the men back to Port Harcourt before releasing them.

***

It was a bright evening, a refreshing breeze seemingly coming from every direction. Everybody in the neighborhood seemed out in their lawns just to savor the coolness of the evening. From where he was, Gabriel could make out human figures in at least six buildings' lawns. He released the toy car and it zoomed off; then he crawled after it on the grass; he was competing with his eleven-month-old son to see who would catch the car first. For the past thirty minutes, he had actually not caught it, but he had not allowed the boy to either. As the boy reaches out to grab the car, he would push it forward and they would start the pursuit again. Then he thought he heard his wife calling. But since he was not sure, he continued his competition.

"Dear," his wife called again.

"Yes Honey," he answered without getting distracted.

"Some people are here to see you."

"Who are they?"

"They didn't tell me. They just said you'd recognize them; that you're expecting them or something."

"Me? I'm not expecting anyone." He then became thoughtful for a moment. "Okay, let them come over," he finally said.

"Okay," she said and turned to go back. She almost collided with one of them, for they were already behind her.

It was then that Gabriel raised his head. The very sight of these four men in grey suits nauseated him. He had actually resorted to calling them predators from hell. By this time they had walked up to him. One of them offered him a handshake. What was he supposed to do about the offer? He took it, though hesitantly. Others did likewise. He waited for his wife to get out of hearing range before talking. "I thought we didn't have business together anymore. So what do you still want with me?"

"We're here to make you an offer," the shortest of them all answered. It had always been the shortest man talking. Gabriel knew that he was their leader and wondered how the most haggard-looking should lead a

45

gang of enormous terrors.

"See, you don't seem to understand my point. Let me repeat myself. I am on a mission and your business conflicts with my objective. We are two parallel lines. Let me be."

As if he did not hear Gabriel, the haggard man asked, "Shall we sit?"

"On the grass if you want; but I see no need." Gabriel did not bother to hide his disgust.

"You will when we're through." They all sat, except Gabriel who remained standing, looking into the distance. When the haggard man saw that his men were all seated, he continued, "We're here, first of all to inform you that this movement, the vanguard of which you are, is stepping on big toes from time to time. Your pointless zeal is consistently making you cross your boundaries and trespassing into the lots of the high and mighty. It is not good. For you, I mean. And this will be your last warning."

"By the way," Gabriel spoke up, "who are these strong men you represent; and in any case, what do you want with me or the movement?"

"Let me start from the second of your questions. We don't have anything to do with the movement. It's a good one, worthy of every support. Let it be forever, or at least until its mission is accomplished. Then to the first question; you can't know the men we speak of unless you work with them. And I think that about answers all your good questions."

"Not satisfactorily though. Work for them as how?"

"Point of correction; work WITH…them. The reason is they don't boss anybody; they associate with people in win-win arrangements. That means that with them is the principle of equity real. Now their course is to attain comfort and then bring as many as are willing in without injury to anyone."

This seemed to irritate Gabriel, and he said, "As you can see, I'm comfortable enough here." He said this with a wave of his hand in a proud show of his residence. "Besides," he added, "I don't understand your idea of comfort."

"Comfort without making trouble for anyone. That's what we mean. What we all want is money; we promise you plenty of it." The haggard man paused. Then he added, "Now I don't like wasting my words; what do you say?"

Gabriel pretended not to understand, "How?"

"By fighting your course in opulence; by making the very people you war against finance the fight; by being diplomatic in your approach to issues." By this time, the man was already on his feet. He edged closer to Gabriel in what may be interpreted as a mild charge. "By living in peace and letting others live in peace too. Now when you join this group, you will know more about the other benefits and the people themselves. I assure you you'd be glad."

To that Gabriel did not have anything prompt to say. He just looked into the distance and seemed to see himself firing away at the very people he was protecting. This, he figured, must be a plot to neutralizing his commitment.

The haggard man continued, this time more direct. "Now, this is the third and final time we'll invite you over." He brought out a card from his breast pocket and said, "I need your written confirmation that you're coming to meet with us tonight." He stretched his hand toward Gabriel, "Here, take this and sign," he said.

Slowly Gabriel turned, faced them, then turned back and looked farther into the distance. His voice came like an echo. "I am not interested in your scam. Now if you will excuse me."

"That's only if you forget the consequence of biting

the finger that feeds you."

"Please leave. And I don't want to see you here again." He said this with an unusual force in his voice.

As his compatriots stood up, the haggard man said, "By the time you discover that you're alone, changing your mind will certainly be too late. Good bye."

Gabriel would have proven the man's last assertion wrong but he was too engrossed in the scenes he was seeing on the horizon. He was pointing his rifle to his father and his grandfather. But he was not about to pull the trigger on the dead. It was their words, said in unison, which burned in his very heart. "So, nothing can be as gratifying as committing oneself to the freedom and well-being of the people he loves. And when all else fails, let the passion for freedom burn even the more."

"Honey," his wife's voice brought him back from the trance.

He swung round to see his wife stooping behind him. "Oh! The men are gone." This, by the tone of his voice, was actually a question.

"Long gone," his wife answered.

"Really? So...fine...so how long have you been here?"

"Quite some time," the woman replied, still stooping.

"I must have been deep in thought then," he said quietly.

"So what's it this time? Those men?"

Gabriel had always acknowledge, though never to anyone, that his wife was sufficiently sensitive and caring, knowing what bothered him at every point in time; she had always being his strength especially when he fainted. "Yes."

"What do they want?"

"Betrayal."

"Betrayal? How?"

"Yes, betrayal. They want me to betray the movement. And they're threatening."

The woman went on her knees. "Honey, please tell me all about this troubling development. Please."

Gabriel did.

When he had finished recounting the encounter, the wife, just for the sake of it, asked him what his answer was.

"No, of course," Gabriel said with a touch of emphasis.

Then she offered him a piece of advice. "Honey, I think you should reconsider. Maybe they're not bad guys as you thought."

Gabriel refused. Rather he suggested that she be moved to a safer place, which she did not want. She argued that she was married to him and was not about to run now that his life was in danger. She then suggested that more boys be brought in to beef up the security at the house. That idea was good. But Gabriel did not mention the possibility of an infiltration of the rank and files of the organization. More people were brought to beef up the security immediately.

**

The news was bad. The militant leader took their gifts of Jeeps, weapons and money and used their own resource to kidnap staffs of their company. And now he knew the position of Jude, their representative, and possibly also knew that the support of Jude and the invitation by the other agents were for the same purpose. This was already too much because he could easily make out the identities of the owners of the foreign oil companies. The main issue was that rather than announce their knowledge of such information, the militants would simply blow up the whole company. And the trio were not going to wait until that happened. He thus needed to be eliminated. But Nsika had just come up with a set up ideas that was going to take the guy to prison before being killed. Just like old times. But Chikodi was apparently getting tired of the approach. We don't have to be that monotonous, he had been arguing for months. "Just kill him and forget about him."

"It's not going to be that easy anymore. Too many people now know the man fronting for us. And somehow there could be a link."

"But, you see, I was thinking that this idea of going through the man at the prison is a complicated one."

Nsika insisted, "The good thing about it is that nothing can be traced to us because even the man doesn't know us. And if anything goes wrong, he won't live to mentions the names of those who give him orders on these matters."

Chikodi paced the study, holding his full cup of wine. He always lost appetite when there was a problem to solve. And it did not matter whether the problem was great or small. He must not eat or sleep while there was something still to be attended to, or at least delegated. At the window, he swung round sharply and announced, "Occam's razor."

"What about it?" Nsika wanted to know, especially when the man who mentioned it seemed not to be saying anything any further about it.

"You know it?"

"No. I don't think so."

"It's a scientific principle. It simply says when there are alternative ways of achieving the same thing, or solving the same problem, as in the case on our hands, choose the simplest."

"So, how does it come in here?"

"I still insist that if we can kill the guy with the gun, the conspiracy idea is not needed at all."

"I'd agree when things are equal. The fronting man in the picture won't let it."

"If he's the problem, why not take him out also and then we won't have to be afraid anymore?"

"Don't forget that Jude is my cousin. I mean, forget it Chikodi; I won't allow that. And by the way, Omuya has not said a word on this." Nsika turned to him, "How do you think we should handle this?"

"I'd say we should do it the way we've always done it. It's safe," Omuya said without lowering the newspaper he was reading. His practice had always been to allow the two men debate issues bothering on human lives and reach conclusions between themselves. Only when they polarized did they require his position to determine what to do. But on other issues, he was always as active as any other.

"So you win," Chikodi said resignedly.

Actually Chikodi had assumed leadership of the group from the start for two main reasons: one, he was the one who birthed the idea and invited others, two, he was on the domineering side of temperament. And the other members of the group knew these. Once, his leadership had been challenged by Nsika and he had reacted by saying that a guest at a meal should not hold the hands of his host. And the topic had never come up again. But he also had always been conscious of his positions; he believed in reasons, and must always present superior arguments, otherwise, he refrained from forcing his sentiment down the throat of his associates.

"It wasn't a contest of who wins in the first place; is it? All that is necessary is that WE win." That was Omuya's standard way of concluding arguments like this. Now it was Omuya's turn to bring up an issue.

"The media guys seem to be up to something. There's a story which tended toward the wrong direction here in this edition of the NATIONAL TRUMPET." He handed the paper to Nsika while Chikodi reached for his own copy.

"Which page?"

"Thirty-seven. First on the InfoTech page."

This was a negative one. "But our CPU is supposed to be the best local brand. What's wrong?"

Omuya had an answer. "It's not the CPU now; it's the laptops. The ram in the last consignment was bad and people have been complaining. But we've told the government not to worry; that it's a small thing. Which they accepted."

It was Nsika's turn to remember something crucial, as they loved to say. "Some guys were reported to be planning to import two ships of laptop from China. Maybe this is their strategy for breaking into the Nigerian market." That, they agreed, was the most probable reason for the bad press the Trio was getting.

Way forward? Omuya suggested that adverts of laptops to run for six months be given to leading media houses.

Nsika added that they be also paid up from the start. By that, the directors of their assembly plant, marketing, and corporate communications would prepare for series of interviews. It was dangerous to bribe reporters; but you could still do many things to earn good press.

Yet another issue of importance: an auto manufacturing company based in China had contacted them. Their latest car brand had failed the most dependable safety test in the world. Unfortunately, they had already mass produced the cars. Now they were desperate for a market to push the products. Nigeria presented them with the largest market opportunity. But they needed established dealers who would take it up.

"That's small," Chikodi cheered. "If they're ready to crash the price, we'll talk with them."

"They are," Omuya assured. "Only that we don't know how bad the cars are."

That word on caution however did not mean anything to Chikodi. "Then we should be on our way to China!"

"But Omuya has a point," Nsika pointed out, still looking doubtful.

"Of course it is when we get there that we'll find out. I believe a car will always be a car anyway; so what is the stress about? We don't have to ride in them anyway."

***

Two days after Gabriel beefed up the security at his home, two police vans came into the compound. The boys who were playing cards when the police vans sped into the compound simply pretended not to notice the men in black and busied themselves with their game. Officers of the law filed out of the vans, guns drawn and made for the house. The boys ignored them.

Gabriel saw the vans through the drawn curtain in his room. That the police knew to come here was a shocker to him. But then, if the strange men did, who else couldn't? The boys would take care of them anyway.

The boys did not. Gabriel sensed this because he expected the men in black to be stopped long before they got too close to the house, an act expected to send the men in black back or lead to, at least, a loud verbal exchange. Or, if the worst comes to the worst, exchange of a few gun shots. None of these happened. So, Gabriel prepared for confrontation, if he would

53

have to. He quickly checked the two pistols in the room, put them out of safety and picked the riffle that had been idle beside his bed for months. He checked that, too, put it at the ready. He then positioned himself and trailed the rifle on the steel door leading to his room. By this time he had already started perceiving movements in nearby rooms. Truly things were falling apart, but he was going to overcome. Then he became afraid for his wife. That thought was cut shut, for just then, the door flew open and his wife rushed in with her gun drawn. Because it was the gun that Gabriel saw first, he opened fire on the intruder. Unfortunately it was his wife that he shot on the head. He dropped the gun and reached for her, forgetting the police and the threat they posed altogether.

"Freeze!" the voice bellowed. "Your hands above your head."

He ignored the voice and continued falling to his knees. But, the hand at the side not visible to the police man was reaching for a pistol. As the police man said, "You're under arrest," Gabriel startled him with a shot. But it only hit him at the right arm. The man's shot came almost at the same time piercing Gabriel's left shoulder.

Just then, three more men in black stormed the room. Gabriel managed to empty his magazine on them. But they wore bullet-proof vests. He felt a sensation on his right arm. He did not have to look at it because just then the hand became limp. "Surrender or I blow your head now! Your hands above your head!"

He was able to raise only the right hand. Thus he was captured.

The boys outside waited for the two vans to leave before cheering. When they were informed the day before that Gabriel had sold out, they did not have to delay in consenting to the mouth-watering offer from the men in suit. Now they would never know the information was false. They headed to the nearest creak where a speed boat would be waiting to take them to the neighboring country. From there they were going to disperse to different countries where they were going to enjoy their booty.

They needed comfort, and they got it.

FOUR

After treatment in a heavily guarded hospital, Gabriel was transferred to the prison. His wife had died, he had learnt. What he found unbelievable however was that the wife, so loving and dedicated, was a mole. Was that why she had had her gun drawn before he shot her? Was that why she had advised him to reconsider the offer made by the men in suit?

At the prison he got his most special welcome from an old man named Henry George and another one named Murphy. Henry had been at the prison for over seventeen years. According to him, he had watched inmates come and go in their thousands. Yet he had not even begun his counting because he had not been tried. And he was sure he was going to be found guilty. At sixty years already, and with not less than twenty-one years of jail term whenever the counting eventually begun, he had resigned to fate. Until the arrival of Murphy the President killer.

Murphy was a celebrated murderer, who, in summary, helped the president of Nigeria to kill all his enemies, and then killed the President himself. Murphy's story had given Henry a small dream, a theory actually. He had shared with the president killer and they had jointly formulated a hypothesis. If the puzzle on their hands was true, and known to the world, generations of Nigerians would at least remember them for good. But the execution had been an unthinkable thing. Murphy had however insisted that if only they could establish contact with one Joseph Meals, things would work out. It was this that Henry was thinking when Gabriel the newest inmate came his way.

"Welcome to our little place," Henry greeted.

"Hi," Gabriel said gruffly. What he wanted was not

a 'welcome'; he needed to know the whereabouts of the dozens of his comrades who were supposed to be here in this prisons. He needed to know how the betrayal was achieved so easily, and without him suspecting. He wanted to see the betrayers punished. But this old prisoner was not going to allow him to concentrate on his plotting. He had already taken a seat beside him.

"Got a minute to... maybe make friends with the oldest fellow around? Actually that's the only way you can survive here if you're meant to."

Gabriel looked at the old man with very sad eyes and nodded slowly, "If you happen to know the whereabouts of some people I thought were here."

"People such as?"

Gabriel hesitated a little. "They were known by their nicknames."

"Nicknames are artifacts here; we preserve them. So?"

"Pepper, Ginger, Alligator, Garlic..." Gabriel stopped abruptly as he saw the old man shake his head pitifully. "What...what's it?"

"Oh, I'm sorry. Er...did you say they were your people?"

"Yes. What's it?"

"So you're also a Niger-Delta militant, sorry for my choice of word." Courtesy did not matter to the old prisoner anymore anyway.

"Yes I am. What about it?"

"It's unfortunate," Henry said, as if to himself.

"How; what's it? Tell me; what is it?"

"It's not necessary that we talk about where they are...for now at least. Instead..."

"Why? I need to see them so that..."

"Would you listen to me? I've been here for a long time. I know all those people and if it's true that you're one of them, then your days may be numbered here."

"Why?"

"Because your predecessors all died in their sleep and I doubt if anybody heard the news outside."

"Oh my God," Gabriel held his head. He had suddenly begun to feel dizzy.

"I'm sorry," the old man said. "I mean there's no better way of relaying a bad news. Just say it as is. Let the worst come to the worst quickly; may be then something could be done to salvage someone else's life. You hear me?" The man continued. "Why am I telling you all these? You may ask. That's because, you see, there may be hope for you. But there're urgent things to do."

Now Gabriel raised his red eyes and fixed his gaze on the old man as he quickly progressed with his monologue. "I've been here for almost twenty years now and my case has not even been decided in court. The implication is that I've met all the Niger Delta youth arrested during the period. Most of them were leaders in the Movement for the Liberation of the Niger Delta. I guess you know that group. Some of them revealed chips of an issue I didn't really start to believe until a man known as the President Killer arrived here about two years ago. You see, I had not been able to make the connection because they all died too quickly. But there may actually be some very big conspiracy going on somewhere. I can tell you that." The old man paused to consider whether to tell the young man the next line of the truth. But then, what did he have to lose? "The conspiracy, as I was saying I suspect is unfortunately being engineered by the bigwigs from the Niger Delta. So it becomes necessary that leaders of the youth groups be either neutralized or terminated."

Just then, the whole revelation began to make sense to Gabriel. His bones tensed, and between clenched teeth and closed eyes he said, "Betrayal!" Then he realized that though there was no conclusion, the old man had stopped speaking. "Ah...er....you...I guess you are right. But...I'm also a leader...of that group. So am I about to die too?"

"Well, you may not. See, to some extent, you people are off the mark in your struggle. The government is not altogether insensitive to your plight; neither are the companies totally inhuman. That much, I know. Your own kins are pouncing heavily on the situation. And unfortunately they want to maintain the status quo. Do you understand what I'm getting at? They don't want the problem to go away. That's where you become a threat. And you can't run away from them because most of them have been where you are. They know how to get you."

Gabriel found all these hard to believe. "You don't mean..."

"You better listen now because I mean everything I'm telling you. Hasn't anybody invited you to a partnership lately?" the old man did not bother to wait for an answer. "Now I, we-Murphy and I, don't want you to die. If you do, we'll have no way of executing our plan. And that means your people will remain in their anguish for a very long time to come. We don't want that to happen."

"Er...can you tell me their names?"

"That will only confuse you the more. It's not yet time for it."

"Okay, how do you think I can get out of this place?"

"Now you're talking. But let me throw your question at you: don't you have an idea how you can?"

"No, I don't."

"You don't have anyone on the staff?"

"No."

"There's a big problem then. You were supposed to

59

make arrangements for such things as this, even if you wish none of you ever gets here. That's a major lapse."

With that resignation, Gabriel's hope evaporated. Unfortunately, it was at that time that the arrival of a prison warden interrupted them. The warden whipped Gabriel sore for leaving his assignment to discuss with a prisoner who had no hope of freedom at all.

But they met again the following day. "Can you pick cuffs?" was the old man's form of greeting. And he was not even looking toward Gabriel.

"Yes," Gabriel replied, also busying himself on his duty.

"How fast? Like twenty in five minutes?"

"Yes... I think so. But why do I need to pick twenty?"

"You better know so. I hear you will be arraigned tomorrow. They will normally execute their evil plan when you return from the arraignment...if you return, actually. So, you see, you must not come back from the court." The elderly prisoner took a cursory survey of his surroundings, and found no threat in sight. "Now this is what we'll try to do: I've not seen their van is seventeen years, but I hear it's the same old Mazda they've been using. It habitually breaks down on the way. They want to top the radiator, they want to add lubricant and all that. I even hear that the exhaust now leaks, which is good news. Now why you will need to pick twenty cuffs is because if you'd ever escape, a whole lot of people will go with you." He espoused the plan and gave a list of people to be taken to court the following day. They swung to action immediately asking those people whether they wanted freedom. Then they told them what to do. "You don't need to panic," was always the concluding line, "it can't be worse even if the attempt fails."

It worked well on the inmates.

Early the following morning, twenty-five prisoners were loaded into a Black Maria ahead of their arraignment. The first thing Gabriel knew was that the list Henry showed him was accurate. He had also observed that Henry's point that only one of the staff on board would be armed was also right. As the van started off Gabriel closed his eyes and prayed silently that the old prisoner was right on every other point. Maybe the fact that the government had neglected the prisons was going to be a blessing after all. Even if the carburetor failed to demand a caress and the radiator failed to ask for a drink they still had a contingency.

Fifteen minutes into the journey, Gabriel had already unlocked fifteen cuffs with a pin he smuggled into the van in his Afro-styled hair. But he had realized that the people were cuffed hands and feet. Meaning that he would need even more time. This was bad news. A very bad one, for some of the people were already feeling apprehensive.

He was rescued however as the fifteenth person mysteriously produced a metal and set to work unlocking faster that Gabriel himself. All the while, the van was roaring as loudly as the almost nonexistent exhaust demanded. Very loud.

The ride to the court was to take about fifty minutes on the average. Forty of those minutes would be on a road habitually avoided by motorists because of its bad state. Good still, the road was boarded by thick bush on both sides. That was where the van was at this time. And it obviously was not going to break down this day. Of all days. "When I count to three," Gabriel whispered, "start!"

The stampede started at the count of one. The staff sitting at the front of the van thought it was a fight, which was not unusual. Just then the van gasped and tripped off. But the prisoners thought it stopped to allow the staffs attend to the supposedly fighting inmates. Before it came to a full stop, the heaviest of the prisoners had thrown his whole weight against the door. Both the door and the bar used to secure it went off their hooks and the prisoner landed on the floor. "Keep still, you bastard!" the armed staff swung his gun between the man on the floor and the open door.

"How many can you kill?" the man on the floor asked and the gun pointed at him. That was to be later interpreted as a mistake on his part as it was intended to distract him. Gabriel leapt onto the man, making straight for his gun. But the impact had already prised the gun out of his hand. Other people in the van rushed out and caught the other staffs before they escaped into the bush. The staffs were all cuffed wrist and feet. Their mouths were tied with scarves and they were locked in the van. Then they pushed the van deep into the thick bush before escaping in different directions.

It would take not less than three hours, Gabriel figured, to locate the van. By then all of them would have been long gone. Or those who were destined to escape.

FIVE

After about two hours of trudging through the forest, Gabriel and four other men got to the bank of a big river. With a good dose of luck, there was a boat at the bank. They saw the owner lying under a tree with what looked like a young girl. Whatever; they boarded the boat and sailed away, westwards for where they came from appeared to be the east.

Twenty minutes later they got to the bridge of a highway. They stopped for some minutes to observe traffic on the highway: it looked like an average of one car in every five minutes. "I think we should get a car here," Gabriel said to his companions. "If they've not found the van by now, they will soon find it and the farther we get the better. They disembarked, taking with them the cutlass and the hunter's gun found in the boat. The boat was left for the kind owner to find, if he's fortunate enough.

With the cutlass they fell a tree and dragged it across the road. The first motorist to come by, it seemed apparent, was blind. He ran over the barricade and lost control. By the time the car came to a stop, it had become useless. The next one made the whole thing easy for them. He probably thought the tree fell of itself, and he drove all the way to the barricade, alighted from the car, surveyed the obstruction and then decided to pull the log off the road. It was too heavy for him. He would have to turn back, or wait for another motorist with whom to remove the barricade.

When he got to the car somebody was already sitting behind the wheel. He did not need to challenge the stranger because just then he saw people jumping down from trees and rushing towards him with clubs. He went on his knees and began to plead for his life.

"You can take the car. There's money in the boot too. Please spare my life in the name of God."

"Stand up and look at us," Gabriel ordered. When the man was on his feet, Gabriel said, "You'll please pardon us because we indeed need your money. But we're not robbers. We'll only borrow your car. We are going to drop it where you'll find it. So do not report it stolen." The man nodded his consent. By this time, the log had been removed. They got into the new Volvo car and sped off.

After crossing three states Gabriel began to relax behind the wheel of the Peugeot 504 station wagon. It was their fifth, and because the owner of this one was taken with them, it was reasonable to go on and on with it. Until they were tired of it. He remembered now that he had not eaten for a long time. They could manage lunch, and, maybe a change of clothing. Gabriel imagined himself in the robe of an Islamic priest. He turned into the driveway of a supermarket. "Where are we going?" somebody wanted to know.

"Let's grab a bite here. And maybe have a change of our clothing" He added too that he needed a break from the long drive. He was already holding a bail of five hundred naira notes.

"Safety first," someone objected firmly. That turned out to be the popular position. But Gabriel insisted that he would go into the supermarket; that they should give him just five minutes if they were not coming with him. He was going to buy snacks for them, he promised.

Somebody else got behind the wheel as soon as he got out of sight.

Gabriel exited twelve minutes later carrying a heavy bag of snacks, only to discover that his companions were gone. He wasted no time looking for them. He stopped a motorcycle and rode to the nearest bus terminus. On the way he found the Peugeot having been run down by a police van. Maybe that was good for them.

At the terminus, Gabriel was the second to the last person to board the Lagos-bound bus. He pretended to be in dire need of comfort on the journey. How much is the fare, he asked the driver. When he learnt how much the fare was, he offered to pay for the remaining one seat; one, because he was going to need the extra space on the journey, two, they needed to save as much time as they could for them not to travel in the night. So the bus set out.

When the people around him began to doze, he began to feel at ease. He reached inside his *agbada* and brought out the notebook that Henry gave him. He needed to make a copy for himself and give the original to a man named Joseph Meals. Murphy also added a personal note to the same Joseph, saying that by that, he was going to establish contact with his daughter. His surprises started from the first page. A list of his tribesmen suspected to be behind the woes of the tribe was presented. Then a theory, which was going to be the assumption driving Joseph Meals' investigation, was written in the pages that follow. God! This whole thing was beginning to make more sense to him. The unprecedented supports, the rekindled interest of the influential ones among his tribesmen, were only facades.

SIX

Joseph had considered the idea of another crazy investigation. It was not to be heard of in his life at least at the moment. Not just because the memories of the last one was still very fresh, but because he was now married; and marriage, he had got to learn by experience, was serious business. He was just going to inform his informant of this decision and apologise.

But this man. He looked at the man again. He had collected the parcel from him, thinking he would read it when he was through assisting his wife in the kitchen. But the man had insisted that he read it immediately; that he was to take certain steps promptly. Then he had read the theory. It was more abstract than one to ever attract his interest. And not really logical. Only that, a name on the list provided on the first page corresponded to one given by Nura Taiwo. But there were more unbelievable aspects of the man's story. He had been claiming to have encountered Murphy, his incarcerated father in-law, recently and that the message was from the prisoner. Was the man himself a prisoner? The answer was no.

So it did not make sense. "If you've not been to prison yourself, how did you meet this man in question?" Joe wanted to know. His instinct already told him clearly that this man was lying.

"I went there to visit a friend, and a warder said I should assist in delivering the letter to you." The man seemed to be avoiding eye contact too.

In that case, Joe said, he would not be able to do anything about the theory. Besides, he was not ready to go to the restive area at this time. Here again, the stranger contradicted himself by claiming to be the one to handle everything in the Niger Delta. For one, he was not supposed to know the content of the letter unless he had torn and read it or he really had met with Murphy. The two possibilities were bad.

"So, who are you?" Mr. Meals wanted to know.

At that point Joyce came into the ante room where the man was being received. She wanted to give her husband a piece of meat. "Oh dear, you have a mail here." He gave her the sealed envelope.

"Impossible!" she said, sinking into a seat beside her husband. "Dad?"

"You believe it?"

"No. but..., wait a minute...the handwriting. It's, it's his." Her hands suddenly dropped unto her laps as she looked at the man more closely. "I don't know. I think I'm getting confused," she finally confessed.

Joseph took the letter from her and read through. When he looked at the stranger again, he said, "Mister, the letter said your name is Gabriel, an estranged leader of one of the Niger Delta youths causing..." he broke off.

The man was on his feet in an instant, apparently debating whether to flee or stay and confess. "No, you don't have to run. Actually you can't go far. This is a heavily guarded home. So again, who are you?"

So the man owned up. He told his story, which, in the light of what was in the note book, now made sense. But it still could be made up.

"I'll let you go," Joseph said. "Give me your contact, and I'll reach you if I later choose to think about all of this."

"Er...I'm sorry, but there's one more thing. I...I...the... Murphy said you could help me with accommodation and feeding till I find my bearing. He said, I should ask that of...er...Joyce...that she should do him that favor."

"Well, I would have believed that if you've been

honest with me. Now I don't believe anything you say. Can you please leave?"

SEVEN

Chikodi looked over at Nsika in the aircraft. The plane would soon begin its final descent towards Beijing's international airport and the Chinese carmakers would be right there at the airport to take them on the twenty-six kilometer trip into the city. The talk was going to be immediate, for the Nigerians had made it clear that they did not have time to spare at all. The implication was then that they were going to be driven straight to their respective hotel rooms where they were going to freshen up and get ready for dinner. The talk was going to take place over dinner. So, Chikodi thought, he was not going to have the opportunity of briefing his associate again.

And he needed so desperately to do that. He leaned over, "Do you really think they're desperate enough?"

"How do you mean?" Nsika seemed not to get the point.

"I mean, we have our proposal, which is what we think is best for us, under the circumstances; how hard do you think they'll cut?"

"Oh, that. Of course I expect them to be selfish, at least at the beginning. That's the primary motive in this terrain. Going by that, I expect them to cut our demands in half, at least, so we'd then begin talks on a level playing ground. What are you really thinking?"

"Exactly what you just said, my friend. We've not considered too seriously what to do should they do that to us. I mean, how hard should we press; at what point should we say to postpone till a future time, or threaten to walk away from their supposed opportunity?"

"Threaten?"

"Yea, threaten, or postpone. We may need that as a weapon, as they're already getting stuck with the cars."

"But do we know whether they've already opened talks with others? We can't take chances with these people."

"You know well that no Nigerian dealer can give them the kind of offer we're giving, in terms of marketing reach, pricing, and even our precedence."

"So?"

"So we can afford to play around with them for some time. Besides, there are not many places where they can dispose of the product with the desired ease. I don't see us losing out on this, if you'll trust me to handle them."

"What's that supposed to mean? You have an idea you didn't share all this while?"

"No; not that. I just believe I have the temperament to handle them; that's all."

"So why am I here if I'm to be an observer?"

"Not passive to the point of absurdity. Not. Not that. Just give me the privilege at every point we need to make commitment. It's going to be sort of a strategy, for us."

Nsika did not seem to follow the logic in the idea. "This will therefore not be a team, really." There was an edge in his voice.

"Don't get me wrong Nsika; we're a team, associates actually, but at points like this, somebody has to take charge as team leader."

"I see," Nsika resigned and appeared to fall into deep thought. From his state, it was clear that he did not want to be disturbed anymore.

Chikodi got the message, and did not bother him again. As he relaxed into his seat, he assured himself that he was going to make a huge success out of the car deal. And whoever was not satisfied with his approach would eventually be appeased by the success. And why should anybody not be happy with him anyway? He had been championing the course of this group for years, and he had not run into any problem as yet. Indeed, he reassured himself, he was doing just fine. Just then the announcement was made over the loud speakers that passengers should return to their seats and fasten their seatbelts.

The time had come for a major breakthrough.

Representatives of the Chinese car makers met Chikodi and Nsika as soon as they passed through customs. It was not difficult for them as both visiting traders looked exactly as they did in their photographs accessible on the internet. The car dealers also knew to identify them by their names-Cheek-hoe-dee, and Ni-zee-ca-ar. They pronounced the names with so obvious a sense of accomplishment, Nsika could not dare correct the bastardisation of his name. "You must be tired by now," the head of the Chinese delegation commented as he lead the train toward the Jeep waiting to take them downtown. In the Jeep, discussion was limited to just pleasantries.

At the hotel, the Nigerians were urged to take four hours to relax after their long flight; after then a vehicle would be sent to collect them. Though their rooms were adjacent to each other, Nsika avoided conversation with Chikodi. Chikodi's attempt at one was frustrated by monosyllabic answers accompanied by trivializing waving of the hand. Thus each man settled in his room, and waited for the time of the meeting.

When the time of the meeting came, Nsika stepped out of his room and joined Chikodi at the corridor. He still appeared to be deep in thought. But something more had happened in the interim: his enthusiasm about the meeting seemed to have evaporated. But Chikodi did not notice this latter aspect. He placed his palm on Nsika's shoulder. "It's going to be alright, I promise, my friend. I know how to handle them," he whispered in Yoruba, a language which though not the native language of either of them, they both understand.

Nsika merely nodded and kept his gaze straight ahead.

Chikodi prompted, "Why, what's wrong? You look worried." He matched his pace.

Nsika passed his briefcase from his right hand to his left and stuffed the right hand into his pocket. "Well, maybe I need to address certain things of personal concern. And…I'll be alright. It's an issue for when I return home. Never mind."

Chikodi knew that it was at best half of the truth, and he was not going to give up so easily, because he thought it was related to the negotiation they were going for. "But I thought that what bothers one bothers all?"

That, of a truth, was a punch below the belt. The trio had become a closely-knitted family sharing everything, good and bad, through the years of their partnership. That, they all knew, had been the bond binding them together. As a matter of fact, they had all come to the agreement that their kind of friendship was many times more binding than any form of oath. But what Nsika was thinking was, really, personal; so much so that he may not even be willing to share it with his wife. "I know," he said. "I know." Just then they got to the car and he stopped talking.

As it turned out, the venue of the negotiation was not far from the hotel. In fact, it was just another end of a single large expanse of land on which were the hotel at one end and the car manufacturing plant at the other. At the front of the manufacturer's administrative building, the driver allowed the Nigerians to alight before asking whether they enjoyed their ride in the company's newest model. Nsika turned and made a cursory assessment of the car's exterior. The interior, he had observed earlier was not bad. But there was certainly more than that. He was going to find out soon.

By the time they got into the conference room, executives of the manufacturing company were already waiting. They rose as their guests stepped into the room, and the Nigerians seized that opportunity to have a dramatic handshake with everyone present. Then they all took their seats and earnestly began to talk.

But Nsika wanted to see the cars first. Or at least some of them. He was not pleased when a dummy version was brought into the room and experts began to give details of the car's make up. Nsika saw Chikodi's brief signal to let things be but ignored it and politely requested that they be shown the real cars.

So the negotiation was suspended for about thirty minutes as the Nigerian traders were shown round the plant. Back in the room, Nsika still had a question.

"Sorry if I appear to be drawing us back. But I just feel like knowing certain details so we'll know what to say. What are the issues with the car brand?"

That question was parried by the man at the head of the desk who said that it only happened to be a new model by a manufacturer yet to assert himself in the world of automobiles. That's all. "It's an issue of confidence. People simply demanded assurance of the highest quality before even using the product at all." This, the man pointed out was hard to achieve. Especially with the cars already mass-produced.

Although Nsika knew that this was not the truth, he stopped pressing, and the negotiation progressed. At this point Chikodi managed to take charge. What was their offering price? He wanted to know. When that information was made available, he simply cut it in two, arguing that so much was still going to be expended on advertisements and sales promotions.

This was obviously far below what the

manufacturers expected. "That is below the cost price," the man at the head of the table said. "Too low," he reiterated looking at Nsika as if he was meant to raise the bid.

"Under the circumstances," Nsika offered, "We may not be able to raise the amount because it is going to be our responsibility to make a market for an unknown product in a market that is already over-saturated. Consider for instance the fact that Peugeot, Nissan and Toyota jointly control over 80 per cent of the new car market in Nigeria. And such upcoming brands like Kia are already gaining acceptance. Mercedes is there for the upper class while Mitsubishi light truck is also not doing badly in the market." He backed this up by pointing out that if the manufacturer had considered their profile, he would have known that theirs was the biggest and widest-reaching car dealer in Nigeria, currently handling more than 60 per cent of corporate sale in the country. And it was going to take that to penetrate the market.

After four hours of negotiations no agreement was reached. But the Nigerian traders promised to discuss the matter when they returned to Nigeria and get back to the manufacturer within another two weeks. Subsequently however, the Chinese would need to visit Nigeria to see the facilities on ground to push the sale of their product. It was unbeatable, Chikodi boasted.

Later that night, Nsika ran into a Nigerian who happened to work with the car maker, and drunk enough to be willing to talk about just anything Nsika wanted to talk about. Since they were still in the hotel bar and neither had anything serious to do again that night, Nsika offered to complicate the man's condition with more bottles. The man was glad. So, what was wrong with the cars? Nsika wanted to know.

Oh, the man exclaimed, there were many things: the

base of the engine did not fit well in its seat. Though this was not evident, a crash test had revealed that it worsens accidents in many fatal folds; the wiring system is said by experts not to be good enough to serve more than two years. The doubt on the braking system in its part was yet to be ascertained; it's there anyway. But the drunk was not even going to bother finding out because he already knew enough to classify the car brand as grade-one-death-knell.

Interestingly, Nsika had a one-touch operate recording facility on his phone, which he used to capture the revelation.

It was an issue for Nigeria, where there was going to be a third person to break any tie. Nsika exchanged telephone numbers and pleasantries with the drunk and promised to keep in touch, though he knew the man would be remorseful in the morning and would never get caught again. He then went to bed, thoroughly exhausted.

***

The meeting this time was holding at Chikodi's home. But to him, there was really nothing to discuss about the car brand. In spite of Nsika's argument and tape recorded conversation, it was a concluded matter. The pricing was good; the cars, at least on the surface, could compete with most of the other brands in its category. And it was for low-income people, particularly civil servants. With its price in the region of that of fairly-used cars commonly patronized by Nigerians, it was going to be hotcake.

Nsika's contention was that they insist on the rewiring of the car, at least. Omuya's idea that if the engine was not equally made to sit well, they were to turn their back on the deal was considered outrageous.

It was an unnecessary precaution, Chikodi argued. Nigerians were prone to accidents for many self-inflicted reasons. So it was not going to be the engine sitting problem causing anybody's accident. Also it had been established that the true causes of fatality on Nigerian roads were bad roads, carelessness, and the fact that drivers licenses were issued not on the basis of driving ability, hence the licensing of people who knew next to nothing about driving. The so-called problems with the car brand, as they were, were not going to deter them from their biggest business deal.

To Nsika's objection, Chikodi explained that a car could always be rewired by the end user. And this coming about two years after purchase, should be no pain at all. Even if it came immediately after purchase, the car was still going to be considerably cheaper than even used ones.

There was, really, no objection. Only profit. And more profit.

Two weeks later, the Chinese car makers travelled to Nigeria to inspect the facilities on ground. Satisfactory. Chikodi also seized the opportunity to drive the three delegates to his night club after conclusion of talks where he introduced them to the nation's minister of transportation as car makers that were destined to make car ownership easily possible for most Nigerians in just days to come.

While the Chinese visitors were left to drink beer, in the company of Nsika, Chikodi returned to the minister to consummate the opportunity he had created. The implication then was that the cars were being imported for the good of the country and therefore had to be imported duty-free. The deal was sealed by a phone call to the President, right in the presence of the minister. Of course they both knew that the president's hands were going to be tied in the circumstances, even if he did not approve of the idea.

Chikodi was aware, and so added promptly that since the cars were coming at a very cheap rate, it would be of a great benefit to civil servants if the president could make a lease purchase arrangement for them such that cars would be distributed at no initial charge, but subsequently payments would be deducted from their salaries. To make the deal what it was meant to be, government was going to give the company an advance payment to facilitate the mass production and importation of the car. That, Chikodi was quick to add, was going to be about the highest achievement of the president, and a strong selling point as he thought of getting another term in office.

To that, the president hesitated, but eventually consented. The government deposit covered up to 60 per cent of the cost of the cars. The remaining would be sourced from the 2 banks belonging to the Trio. And they knew that the banks were well able to raise the huge amount. The two of them had just returned from the capital market where they had raised a combined 55 billion naira through initial public offers, a success that had made both banks two of the biggest and most promising in the industry. At least according to available data. Now that they were meant to do business with their sumptuous capital, credit had become readily available to the patrons. But much more was needed than the banks could offer, even with their newly amassed capital. What could be done?

Deposit. It was Chikodi's idea. Bank deposits could be borrowed for the period. The mild protest by the MD of one of the banks on ethics was rendered trivial by the argument that no auditor was going to ask for financial papers during the period as the financial year was just commencing. Besides, unless there was an apparent disaster looming, customers were not all going to ask for their money at about the same time. Some were always going to bring in more money while some withdrew, and with the media rave going on and renewal of people's belief in the system, nothing was going to go wrong. At least not in the nearest future. So it was a perfect idea.

EIGHT

The news came as a rude shock. A mail from a reporter, claiming he had information about the health of the cars that were just imported from China and imposed on civil servants in the nation. His request though not really a request was that he was giving the car dealers a chance to speak on their side of the issue; would they?

They were in Omuya's study while the issue came up, and Nsika's first response was *what were they going to say?*

Omuya did not wish to contribute to this matter, or just did not know what to contribute. He watched as the duo strategized. It was only one newspaper, and it was doubtful that the reporter in question could go so far without hard fact. They could ignore his request; pretend they did not see it, until he makes physical contact which he was sure to make shortly. At least until then he was not likely to go to press. Whenever he did show up, they would be prepared to make him an offer. Besides the director of their auto sale company would also make him see that he was on a collision course with the whole nation– the constitution actually– and would therefore need to thread softly.

In the mean time they were going to bombard both the print and electronic media with adverts rich enough to win the hearts of the citizens. With good money coming from adverts, media interviews would be easy to earn. And that was going to present them the opportunity to win completely the hearts of the people in their campaign. Punch line: this was just a prelude to the establishment of the first car manufacturing company in the country. And with the company's demand for labor, millions of people were going to get employed within a few months.

Whatever the reporter did after that was only going to amount to scooping a cup of water from an ocean.

It was perfect logic. So they swung to action from the study and ordered the auto sale company to invite press men to a conference holding in two days.

At the press conference, laptops were distributed to reporters to record and take notes, and afterward take away. Cameras as well as latest telephone handsets were also distributed for the same reasons. That kept everybody busy for the first fifty-five minutes. Then came the briefing proper, which lasted eight minutes. But for another thirty minutes, advertisement materials and upfront payments were given to all media houses present.

And then the journalists were released to perfect the image laundering job. Anybody who dared to go against this arrangement would soon realize that whoever shakes a stump is only shaking himself.

**

Even if Joseph had been interested in having anything to do with the man from prison, the health of his wife was not giving him the room. It was as if they were carrying the pregnancy together. Joyce' bed rest had now relapsed to full-time, requiring that her husband remain at her side almost all day, practically carrying and feeding her, and even reading the Bible to her. Her condition had simply put her in control of the man; and any attempt to dodge was being read as an act of wickedness, or at the very least, insensitivity. After running errands all day he was going to fall into bed in the night exhausted. All he made do with in the name of news now was the highly abridged and doctored version of issues fed to the populace by the television stations. Nothing, even on the web, presented him with more detailed and accurate analyses as when he had gone out to see things for himself. As such, Joseph had lost touch with many current issues in the polity.

Nevertheless, he gave kudos to the reporters in his employ. At least they stood out. Sitting beside his wife on the bed, Joseph read his mail on his phone. "What!" he shouted suddenly.

Joyce was startled and Joseph realized immediately what he had done and apologized. "I'm so sorry," he said over and over again. "But my dear, you see, we're sitting on a keg of gunpowder." He knew Joyce did not understand his point, so he continued. "Romeo just mailed me from the US that some cars were about to flood the Nigerian market that were going to result in carnage in a very short while."

Joyce closed her eyes in fury. "So how does that affect my baby and me? Why doesn't he tell the Government straight away?" With the pregnancy, she had become completely irrational.

"You see, my dear, he can't. It's not the kind of things you tell Government. You won't understand." Joseph finished reading the mail, and stepped out of the room consciously moving out of his wife's hearing range. Then he placed a call to the man holding forth for him as editor of his magazine.

"What was it that you said about the cars about to be imported from China?"

"The importation has already started. And serious adverts have also started to run in almost all media houses. I mean these are the latest facts ..."

"You haven't answered my question yet; what is the issue with them?"

"I gathered that the cars are defective and not so safe for use. But from the look of things government has decided to force them on civil servants. This is yet to get out, but that looks irreversible. I've contacted..."

"Alright," Joseph interrupted the editor, "could you come over and brief me properly?"

"Okay, I'll be there shortly."

The man got to Joseph's door so quickly Joseph had to ask if he was almost there at the time of the telephone conversation. But of course he was not. He was only blessed with a driver who drove as if death was at his heals. The briefing took place right at the door. But the first realization to hit Joseph was that by making a hasty contact with the dealers of the cars in question, the editor had already dealt a severe blow to the investigation. Albeit not without redemption.

For a start, however, Joseph instructed the editor to now keep the investigation underground until concrete evidence was got. And that was going to be difficult as things now stood. But they were going to get it.

As the editor turned and walked on the balls of his feet toward his car, Joseph began to think about Nura Taiwo. May be it was his turn to look for the old man. Just before he shut the door, he saw a familiar figure walking toward the house. Without thinking of his last encounter with the ex-prisoner, he went out to meet him, extending his hand as he approached the man.

"So, how are you doing today?" he asked as if they had been acquaintances for long, and as if the man's character had no blemish whatsoever.

Even the man noticed the change of attitude immediately. He took the hand extended to him and replied, "F–fine," obviously puzzled.

Joseph examined the man closely. The truth was that he now needed somebody to run errands on dangerous terrains; but then, this did not seem to be the suitable person. He was not likely to succeed in resisting the temptation anyway, especially considering the fact that his presence may be a plus to security.

"So have you now sorted yourself out?" Joe would

have added his name if he still remembered it.

The man looked away. "Not quite. I've been putting up under a bridge at Oshodi, among derelicts...which makes me one of them actually."

"What!" Joseph was sincerely surprised. "Do you realize how dangerous that is, Mr....?"

"Gabriel," the man imputed. "I did, but that is the only option open to me. And that's why I'm here again; to see if you've reconsidered, or if you'd like to ask Murphy, somehow."

"Well, I think it will make more sense if you tell me about yourself now. I should think you're here because you're ready to do that."

So right where they stood, Gabriel told of his crusading role and the betrayal which he never suspected. The worst thing about the betrayal was that even his wife colluded with the enemies all the way. He also told of the shock of finding that every Niger-Delta crusader who had gone to prison before him had been killed, and only he, with the help of Murphy and another aged prisoner had escaped. He told of the bitter realities of the major financiers of their crusade also constituting the greatest opposition. And that opposition was lethal.

Joseph could see the pain in the man's voice as he spoke; he could tell now that the man was to a very large extent, telling him the truth.

"So what do you plan to do now that you are all alone, and a fugitive?"

"I now believe that the battle cannot be won by violence. Neither can it be won by confrontation. I believe that the pen, especially of a journalist, is mightier than the sword. I need somebody who has the means to fight the battle on intellectual grounds, while I supply every piece of information needed. I tell you, there's nothing I cannot get. In spite of what I've been through, I'm still committed to the crusade. And there are one or two people who are also still very committed. I can find them…I'll find them." The man suddenly broke off and looked straight into Joe's eyes, for the first time. "Murphy told me of your pedigree, that you've done something greater, and this would only be a small thing for you to do." Now the man seemed to be looking beyond Joseph. "But…he also said I could as well forget it if you decline. I may not get any other person who is passionate enough about Nigeria to undertake this…in my circumstances." He looked into Joe's eyes again, biting his lower lip. He had finished all he had to say.

Joseph cleared his throat loudly. "I see," was all he said as he made eye contact with the ex-prisoner. "Even if I wanted to undertake this, it's already a false start, and you know that. Strange as it may appear, but my wife's state is the first barrier, while the consequence of being discovered to be connected to you is the second. And a more serious obstacle for that matter." Joseph had suddenly become more thoughtful than he was even when he was engrossed in his most absorbing assignments. "This is what I will do: I'll give you money to settle your accommodation, and feeding, at least until you are able to find your own way. And I expect you to do that pretty soon. Then I wish you well."

Then the man shocked him with his spontaneous reply. "Mr. Meals you really don't understand where I'm coming from. I don't need assistance to survive; accommodation as you have conceived it will only make me vulnerable. And with the bad guys taking the money from the government and getting applauded by the very people they are shortchanging, my life can only be more miserable than that of a prisoner. What I need is the partnership that will uncover all these wrong. What I want is justice for the Niger-Delta; what I desire is restoration of the region; what I crave is peace, what I desperately need now, is more than money, it is help…your help."

Joseph saw right in the man's eyes pleas. And, oh! God, he had been hooked again. He had already identified with the man. His passion had been fired up; he would not be able to refuse this.

***

In his usual manner, Nura Taiwo was up early. Joseph Meals had called the previous night that he would be coming to discuss the project at hand with him in the morning. Finally, when he was beginning to think Joe was not going to fall for it this time, the reporter himself had called, asking for a meeting. So Nura had simply lost his sleep, and instead prayed overnight. After all, he had become a Christian, and a Christian, if he is true to his calling, says father Trevor Huddleston, is an agitator. So praying overnight was part of the agitation. Thus Nura's prayer had been inspired by gladness and a fresh hope borne out of the reporter's declared interest and driven by anger that the enemies were in control of his country.

Nura opened the gate for Joe, as usual, and watched as the reporter drove his ridiculous Volkswagen Beetle all the way to the parking lot. "If you would ever trust gifts from anyone again, I should wish to give you a better car than this, in exchange actually, just to ensure you never get to use this jalopy again."

"But you see," Joseph countered matter-of-factly, "You want to throw me into loneliness then, because this car has become my best professional companion, sharing both bitter and sweet memories with me. No other car can be like it. Even my wife can't keep me company like this nice little car." He left the door of the car open and walked quickly to the man for the routine handshake.

As if prompted by the mention of Joseph's wife, Nura inquired, "I hope you're not finding marriage too challenging? You see, women can be selfish, and unrealistic."

"You're right, chief. It's quite challenging."

The man led Joseph into his dining room where breakfast was already served. "I didn't ask what you'd like because I know all the menus you can't resist." The elderly man motioned for him to sit, and he took his usual seat at the head of the dining table. He stretched his hand as if he were going to draw his plate, then stopped and asked, "By the way, you haven't said why you wanted to see me." It was more than a mere comment.

Joseph promptly gave him his premeditated line. "Oh! To find out the reasoning behind what you suggested to me the last time. To see if there are now more facts with which I can begin to consider it."

"My goodness! You mean that's where you are, many weeks after?"

"But you know that fire doesn't burn you twice in error. Besides, every marriage comes with its troubles; and one just has to pass through those troubles. I now believe that philosophy, that is."

"Good of you anyway. So where do we start this time?" Nura now drew his plate and began to serve himself. "From a recap of the last time?"

"If you don't mind." With that came Joseph's turn to help himself to the food. So he got into that with all seriousness.

Nura took a few bites of toast bread garnished with more sauces than Joseph thought necessary and stepped it down with a few sips of coffee. He then placed the cup down rather loudly, and looked intently at his visitor. "The last time you came here," he started, "I told you of certain business men who had…have short changed the whole country. But they are so clever it will require an act of journalistic genius to piece the facts together in a way convincing enough to nail them." Nura took another sip. "That's the recap."

"Yes sir."

Nura was still speaking. "And I gave you certain names; some of politicians, some of top-ranking civil and public servants colluding with them. One of those is a key figure on the stock exchange; another is a Director-General at the ministry of finance. But now I know you did not work on that list. You probably don't believe it, and I don't blame you."

"You see, I confess there is still something about this issue that is yet to click on my mind. That's why I'm back. Maybe more, and perhaps fresh details can help." By this time, Joseph had forgotten his food.

Nura adjusted in his seat and offered, "Fortunately, I think there is something fresh." He reached to a desk close by him and brought a laptop. He pushed the tray of food away and hit the start button on the computer. The screen came up instantly, and he continued with what he was saying as if there had not been a break. "An auto sale company has just come on the scene, with a big promo. They are importing a new car brand from China. They're pumping real money into their sales promotion." The man leaned on the desk to get closer to Joe. "Interestingly, in spite of their seeming lack of precedence, Government is said to have paid them for more cars than they can possibly import in another one year. And these cars, Government intends to force down the throat of civil servants nationwide. Lease purchase they call it. But there must be more to it than that." The man lowered his voice, but even so, anger was evident in his tone. "The car brand is unknown, probably untested, where we have Peugeot assembling here in Nigeria, where we have Nissan and Toyota, two of the most dependable brands in the world." The man sat upright. "Do you really get what I'm driving at, Mr. Meals?"

Joseph did not even notice the sudden formality. His mind had been fired up. Now, this was a real situation. And he knew that his fragile peace had finally been shattered. He nodded, and looked straight into his host's eyes. He traced his index finger along the tip of the glass he had just used in drinking water. No word came out of his mouth.

Nura knew the implication of that posture. And he also knew how to put words into people's mouths, or at least how to get them talking. "Do you think it will be worth your effort?" He asked this question closing the lid of his laptop and actually pushing the machine away.

Joseph's voice was barely a whisper. "It will be tough. But I think…" he broke off, and instead asked, "Do you see any connection between these people and the unrest in the Niger-Delta?"

Nura considered this question a minute and replied candidly, "Initially I suspected that; but now I'm not sure. I won't be surprised?"

Joseph suddenly felt a little hazy and he relaxed in his seat, closing his eyes for up to one full minute. When he opened his eyes, Nura was looking curiously at him, something close to alarm in his eyes. He saw that clearly. Thus with a feigned smile, one Nura was not likely to believe, he said, "I'll do my best."

"I trust you. You know, you look to me like the only hope of this country." He stopped speaking again. He was beginning to think Joseph's reactions unusual. "Don't you think you need some rest, or something?"

That was actually his way of saying what he did not want to say directly. Joseph conceded to that. He however added that he might even need to see a doctor, especially now that he saw himself going into another stressful investigation. His health needed to be sound.

"Please do," Nura counseled. Then they both tried to return to their breakfast. It was late, for something more emotionally engaging had overridden whatever desire for food they might have had. Thus Nura had the table cleared as he walked the reporter to his car.

Church. The word hit Joseph like a heavy blow. He needed to get to a church. Maybe it was prayer that he really needed at the moment. Incidentally, he remembered an advert he had heard lately, of a crusade holding somewhere not too far from where he was at present. But he was not sure of the time. The last time he attended church was when things had almost gone out of control. Maybe it would be wise now to go before even starting a new assignment. That, he told himself, might be the assuring punch he needed. He was going to attend the crusade.

He drove to the next junction and turned left. If he was right, that street should lead him to a place just behind the venue. He was right, so he merely drove round the compound and was at his destination.

At the venue of the crusade He was told that the grand finale of the program had just ended. Joseph just went numb in his seat. He heard the young girl attending to him call out just to conclude the information she was giving, but he could not respond. The girl called again, sounding actually alarmed.

Joseph did not respond. Thus the girl called out to the people clearing the dirt at the venue of the crusade. From then on Joseph did not know what happened. He just opened his eyes under a tree two hours later, people praying earnestly all around him. Because he witnessed the progression to this point up to a point in his numbness, he did not have to ask anyone what he was doing at the strange place. Rather he said, "Pastor. Where is pastor?"

"Which of the pastors?" somebody wanted to know.

"Any of them. Could even be the Evangelist, the Reverend; any one." As Joseph said this he realized he was probably going out of his mind. "Where is he?"

"Here I am brother; what's the matter?" a chubby man bent beside him and placed a crisp palm tenderly on his cheek. As he did that Joseph shuddered and laid still for a while. The man kept his eyes on him.

"I need to see you alone Pastor." Just then, other people around left them and he struggled to sit up. With the help of the pastor, he managed to do that, now resting against a tree. "What is the way forward?"

Pastor was at a loss. But experience had taught him how to handle such situations. He said nothing, but looked at the man still. "Tell me pastor. Tell me the way forward."

"My brother," the Pastor said and paused briefly before continuing. "You've not yet told me at which point you are stuck, and what the problem really is." Pastor blinked rapidly, as if he was doing it for effect. "Would you mind doing that?"

"I'm stuck at many points, Pastor," Joseph declared. "I'm a successful man. A very successful Lawyer and Journalist. I'm Joseph Meals." He paused expecting to see recognition on the man's face. In deed he saw it. "But I'm not fulfilled. Please Pastor, do not tell anyone this. I gave all that I am to my work. And I see results. The whole world sees them actually. But there is still a sort of emptiness within me. I tend not to appreciate myself in any rate close to how people do." Pastor merely nodded, and allowed him to continue. "Then, Pastor, I thought marriage was exiting. I thought it was going to fill the void and make me complete. It is actually just starting. But my wife's pregnancy has ruined everything. She seems to be losing her balance. Pastor, my wife is becoming mentally unstable, worried by her father in prison, and the dangers that may not be in another fifty years. My sister is now a widow. Her husband died…because of me. Nobody has accused me of that, but everybody knows it. She's beaten in life already; she's a loser so I'll become a winner. My successes have come at very great prices, what can I do; Pastor what can I do? I'm…I'm…I'm." when words stopped flowing from his mouth, he kept quiet and closed his eyes.

Then Pastor cleared his throat and said "Let's pray." He offered a short prayer for revelation and guidance and said "Amen" himself at the end of it, not expecting Joe to contribute anything, possibly because he felt the journalist may not. Then he sat beside Joseph and placed his giant-print Bible on the floor right in front of him. Joseph was to conclude less than two minutes into the Pastor's counsel that he deliberately placed the Bible where he was going to be able to keep his eyes fixed on it. "Brother," the Pastor began. "Although you've only told me a fragment of many things, I can see beneath the many layers. Let's begin here: Are you a Christian?"

"Yes. My name is Joseph."

"I didn't mean it that way, actually. Is there any point in your life when you consciously said you're surrendering to Jesus?"

Oh! Joseph understood perfectly, and he knew what the answer was. At least, not likely to be in the affirmative. He looked to the opposite side of the pastor's, "I…I don't think so. No."

"I think it's time you did that, brother." In the next three minutes, he lead Joseph through the process of conversion, and then congratulated him. Then, he said, as if he had authority over the whole earth, that concerning the issues troubling Joseph, it was well. He was still going to meet him for counseling, but, his immediate pronouncement was that God had taken over. Just like that. Then he prayed, as it seemed, only for Joseph's father-in-law. Obviously this Pastor did not know Murphy's offence, or he failed to make use of his senses, because he simply commanded the release of the prisoner. Joseph did not bother to even waste his 'Amen' on that. As usual, Pastor, did not need his 'Amen' because he said it himself.

It was when Joseph opened his eyes that he realized that Pastor had stood during the prayer. The chubby Pastor extended his hand toward Joseph to lend him a support as he rose to his feet. "Put your mind at rest," he said, "God is in control." He said this with such confidence as suggested he did not believe there was a problem in the first place and gave Joseph his card and urged him to call at the church for further prayers and counseling.

Joseph could not bring himself to telling his wife what happened to him at the crusade ground. Why should he, especially when after all the embarrassment, the Pastor clearly demonstrated the passiveness of his mental faculty. But then, he could not deny a fact; he had finally unburdened himself, shared his secret emptiness with somebody, though under influence of what he might never understand. Somehow the episode had lightened him, and now he was more willing to embark of Nura's exploration. He had already thought of how to balance things. He was going to set up a makeshift office in the garage, so he could hear his wife when she called and still run the investigation without any interruption. From there also, he could meet with the two people who were going to be his associates without necessarily violating his own privacy.

It was at his desk in the improvised office that he now sat, strategizing with his editor. The editor was going to handle the paper works, Gabriel was going to handle the physically challenging aspects yet to be articulated, while Joe himself would make the physical contact with the people concerned. Telephone correspondence was going to be forbidden, while encrypted e-mails would be used in extreme situations. The editor was to always deliver reports verbally. Nothing was to be written, at least by the other parties to the investigation.

How Gabriel's part was going to be handled was yet to be determined. But Joe knew it was not going to be easy because the guy was a fugitive, or even a crime personified. Joseph allowed the editor to go so he could put the initial paper works together hence setting direction for the investigation. No sooner than the editor had gone had Joe himself got on the road. He had to see Gabriel. He needed to talk to the fugitive; though he did not know where or how he had come into the picture at present, he knew somehow the guy was going to be needed. Then for a fleeting moment the emptiness within came to mind, and he made a note to maybe see the chubby pastor soon. If only to now pray concerning the investigation, for he eventually did not achieve that when he went to the crusade ground.

The figure caught his attention when it was almost too late. Like a derelict savoring the shade and coolness offered by riverside trees on a hot afternoon. Maybe the tree was big enough to offer such luxury; but nobody, not even an insane person, was allowed to come this close to Joe's home. And he was just going out, leaving only his helpless wife in the house.

As Joseph alighted from the car, his right hand stuffed into his pocket, holding a gun, he got a feeling that the person was actually waving to him. Then the person got up and walked rapidly toward him.

"What!" Joseph was visibly furious. "What are you doing here?" he roared rather than demanded.

The outburst forced Gabriel to stop in his track. "I'm sorry if I offended you," he apologized. "I…I was just hungry and tired…and a little afraid of going to the open in the day time. I'm sorry." The man had now started a cautious approach.

"Sorry? You attempt to compromise my security and you're sorry? What kind of apology is that? Tell me." For the moment of outrage Joseph forgot that it was actually this man that he was going to find. And that without even a clue of where he was. The truth was that Joseph was beginning to see him as a mole, a planting of another lawless principality. And if that was the case, what was he supposed to do? "Look," Joseph bellowed, "What is your mission here?" As he said this, there was a stir in the grass just about seven meters to his right. Joe swung round, his pistol at the ready. At the sight of the gun, Gabriel went flat on his belly. Then the wild rabbit ran back into the bush.

"Look," Joseph bellowed again, "you've already become a nuisance around here. Now leave!" He said this pointing toward the exit.

Gabriel rubbed his palms together in plea, but Joe got the more furious. He pointed the gun at him. "Now go! Get out of here! I will shoot you now!" Joseph's eyes, as it were, were already emitting fire.

Then Gabriel surprised him. He raised his hands and came a little closer. "See," he said loud enough for him to hear, but not enough for the person now standing behind him to hear. "If you won't help me then its better you be the one to kill me; I'm going to die anyway. Shoot. Shoot me or help me."

At that point Joseph thought he saw desperation in

the man's eyes. Or was it in his voice? Maybe both.

"Joe!" the person called from behind and Joseph froze, certain that the weapon he held was going to stir a lot of trouble in his home for many years to come.

He did not bother to face his wife who must have exerted a lot of energy to get here in her situation. "What are you doing out here my dear?" He tried all that he could to keep the anger out of his voice. But he knew himself that he did not succeed.

Joyce ignored that fact anyway. "Nothing; I heard your voice and knew at once that you might be in danger. So I came out here and there you are ready to kill…"

"Is that why you have to expose yourself to this danger and the stress in your condition?"

"If anything hurts you here it will soon get inside to hurt me anyway. And do you realize your voice is not at all friendly?" Joyce took the gun from him and looked straight at Gabriel, and changed the subject. "I can't believe he's still around."

"Precisely. Maybe he has to return where he came from." Joseph took Joyce's hand and lead her toward the house. "But you didn't need this risk," he said, now friendlier in tone.

"It's no risk at all. At least for someone who has watched people killed before, and has almost got killed herself." She lowered her voice even more. "He's following us. Can we ever get him off our back?"

Joe stopped, put his hand in his pocket, and gave some money to Gabriel. "There's a cheap hotel three streets from here. Lodge there. Stay in door and get yourself some food. I'll get to you."

The man took the money, thanked Joseph and pleaded not to be forgotten. As soon as Joe got into the house, he tried to caress his wife and make her relaxed and comfortable in bed. This took a lot of time and patience. But he eventually achieved it. Then he went into his office to call Nura Taiwo on a safe telephone. He wanted the old man to get him the telephone number of the prison where Murphy was and possibly a senior staff there. It would be nice if the staff was alerted that he was going to call and was going to ask to speak with the man called Murphy. Privately, of course.

All this was arranged within forty-five minutes. So Joseph got through to Murphy. He put his phone on speaker as he talked very personal things with him for the first ten minutes. Joyce recognized the voice instantly and gave a nod. Then as the prisoner sensed that Joseph was going to bring up the subject, he feigned a level of spirituality. "Least I forget, my in-law, you will see a wise wayfarer with a message of hope, asking for help. He is true; and if you help him, he will help you. So will you succeed together." Murphy smiled as he said this. Nobody within the prison could decode this as they were only going to think that the confinement was driving him crazy. And if they were eavesdropping, they were sure to surface now to take their phone from him before he damaged it. A man out of his mind was always accounted dangerous, especially when incarcerated.

That was exactly what happened. So all that Joseph heard next on his end was, "Give me the phone, you this mad man!" And he was afraid that piece of information may not be good for his wife who was still sitting close by.

But even Joyce understood the message.

***

Joseph studied the man again. He did not need to tell him of the conversation with Murphy which certified him as true. Joseph had already decided on that before coming down to interrogate the ex. And for security reasons, he had him dress in a neat conservative outfit and wait for him at a local food canteen. There they ate amala over casual chats; then took a bottle of beer each and went to sit under a tree behind the canteen, a place where people coming and going were not going to see them. When Joe had made certain that nobody could eavesdrop, he began.

"These people you allege to be hurting the Niger-Delta under a guise; can you tell me about them?"

Gabriel was instant, beginning with a point of correction. "They are not alleged. They are actually robbing the region." Joseph was going to protest that until they had been pronounced guilty by the court of law, they were not to be condemned yet but Gabriel preempted that and quickly continued. "And unfortunately, they are getting praised for it." Gabriel shook his head sadly. "They are getting honored for their dishonorable acts perpetrated in secret."

By this time Joe had resorted to listening, after all he was to listen if he was to gain anything useful. His tutelage of the fugitive, he concluded, was only going to be counterproductive. He nodded, looking straight into the man's eyes. He actually wanted to make eye contact but the man avoided it. Rather he fixed his gaze on the beer bottle in his hand as he spoke.

"You see, they know the area. They are rich, actually making their fortunes off their people's misfortunes. They usually start by pretending to be active in the crusade. But they only do that to gain attention of the multinational oil companies and the government. The moment they get that, they sell out. Unfortunately the society is such that wealth sudden or not, clean or not, has the means of transforming people overnight. They then harp on their new bogus status and make themselves liaison persons with government and oil companies. They are the only ones who could stand before government so they negotiate on behalf of the communities. They reach agreements and publicize them. But little or nothing of whatever is agreed upon gets to the people. And since they are the only ones who can be heard and believed outside, we have no voice whatsoever." He looked at Joseph, "And you see, our other approach is grossly unpopular."

Joseph cleared his throat, and then paused for a little while to see whether the ex was still going to speak. He was not. Then he asked, "These people you are talking about, do you know them?"

"Of course, I know them. Some of them wanted to recruit me but I rebuffed their advances. So they set me up. That's how I got to prison, and was meant to be killed in custody before Murphy helped me to escape."

Joe's curiosity was aroused about the set up, but thought that could wait till a more appropriate time. "And you have names?" he asked.

"Of course."

"And you can prove this well?"

"Of course."

"I mean, give me facts, get people who will testify, and establish the connection with both government and the oil companies?"

"Of course. I've actually come to believe that that is a better way of fighting this course. I will do those things you are saying."

"How easy and fast can you do them if I tell you to?"

At this point the man was thoughtful for a moment. "You know I'm a wanted man. I will have to move cautiously, avoiding both government security operatives and those of the enemies. I will also have to convince people before they testify. If I will need photos, it will be more difficult. But I can do it. And I will try to be fast." As Joe was about to talk, he cut in and added, "I will need many things for the job."

"Leave whatever you need to me. I can afford a small car, a camera, a tape recorder...even a laptop computer if you know how to use it. My concern is your safety and my confidentiality. By that I mean the moment words get out that I'm up to something along that line, they will come tooth and nail after me. They won't ever let the project take off, let alone succeed." Joe looked into the man's eyes again just to drive home this last point. "And, Gab, you're going to determine all that. Whether this investigation succeeds or not depends on how you handle things when you're on your own."

"If you know the nature of our operations you will know that I'm not a person to be careless with issues like this. And you know that it's either I succeed or there's no world for me to actually live in. They won't let me. My battle is now more personal."

Joseph noticed that the man said this clenching his fists and twisting his lips in a way that contorted his whole face. "Alright then. Let me have the names." He asked this, knowing well that he did not really need to. A list was enclosed in the letter from Murphy. But asking firsthand from Gabriel would allow him to also ask about the people's background however sketchy the ex could give.

Gabriel gave him the names offhand. As soon as he made an end of mentioning the names, Joseph ventured, "What can you tell me about them, or at least some of them?"

The first one Gabriel was going to comment on was a man named Nsika Isaiah who hailed from the same village with Gabriel. "Hopes were high when he was at law school that he was going to take care of the legal aspect of the crusade. Immediately after his graduation he seemed to go into that. But it was short lived. And he became rich instantly. In a short while he joined a group that we believe to be behind oil bunkering. But we've never been able to prove anything. The man is very connected. He also sells computers. It was rumored that he was into many things. But you won't find that link between him and any of those businesses. We however found his name as executive director in a few companies in Corporate Affairs Commission's register." Gabriel's group searched for more concrete facts for years and realized they were only wasting their resources. So they gave up. Also, with issues relating to the Niger-Delta, Nsika was always acting by proxy. He never made any direct contact with the region. "But I'm positive he is a major problem to the region. I'll try my best to prove it." Gabriel promised.

Joseph was now burning inside. The name Nsika Isaiah was already mentioned to him by Nura Taiwo, though in line with a completely different issue. But now Joe was already thinking that the issues might actually be connected. That, he knew, would make the investigation more tedious, but more importantly, more dangerous.

In the mean time, Joseph told Gabriel to move to another hotel where a car to be bought under a phony name would be delivered along with other necessary equipment. Whatever he would have to do would also be communicated to him then.

It turned out that up to sixty per cent of the preliminary investigations would have to be carried out in the Niger-Delta region, and Gabriel was going to go to work immediately. His schedule was a tight one, because, Joseph explained, the longer the investigation, the more likely it was for confidentiality to be compromised.

On Sunday afternoon Gabriel put his luggage into

the boot of the old modeled Nissan Maxima given to him and got in behind the wheels. He understood the rationale behind the choice of the car. Big enough engine for speed if needs be, old enough model not to be too attractive, and dull enough color to be seldom noticed when passing. He drove all the way to Port Harcourt where he intended to meet with a fellow crusader who in his case only narrowly missed a disastrous set up and was now retired from violence due to the attending injuries. But never from the fight. He would be glad to know that Gabriel had escaped from prison. And would be willing to offer assistance. Then he hoped to go to Calabar where he was to get people in the villages to testify to what they had suffered in the hands of their own people.

He hoped to return with something sufficiently damning in one week.

In Lagos Joseph concentrated on the car sellers. Though he was already feeling a whiff of suspicion that there was going to be a link with the Niger-Delta case, he had not had the courage to make it a major premise in his investigation. He just continued to find all that he could. He searched on-line for auto crash test. For several hours, all he found was on popular car brands, and those striving for a place in the global marketplace; those that succeeded, and those that did not. And there were thousands of pages on them. He continued to trawl. Cemento, as the car he was concerned with was called, was never mentioned. Not even in passing. When he became sure that his search was bothering on hopelessness, he altered his search phrase to 'cars manufactured in China'. Almost all the major brands appeared in the results. More frustrating was the fact that all the materials that came out in the other searches, it seemed, reappeared again. So he travelled the same hopeless road all over again, until he was fed up.

Then it occurred to him that Romeo in the US could be of assistance here. He sent him a mail asking if it was not going to be trouble for him in his busy schedules. Never, Romeo replied immediately and even asked that they chat so he could get detail about the quest. That they did for another two hours. Through the chat, Joe was as open as he could; after all, this was Romeo who gave him the all important document needed to nail the late President who happened to be his own father. When Romeo was satisfied with the information available, he promised to work on it and get to Joe within a few hours. And in case something came up more quickly than anticipated, Joe was to stay close to the internet.

Romeo had implied that he was going to contact a client who worked with an auto magazine which also happened to be one of the foremost auto rating agencies in the world. He was positive something would come out of there. What, neither of them could tell.

As it turned out, the first batch of data came only in twenty minutes. Cemento might exist as a variant of a failed brand named Macedat, which failed certain safety tests. But the search was progressing. At that point, Joe stopped his own fruitless search and just kept his mail box opened, and fixed his gaze on it. He did not do that for long. The reasons, a follow up mail revealed, were safety and wiring. A candid commentator was even reported to have written the brand off as not fit for any living thing. It was fated to be a murder box.

But all this had been, by a method yet to be familiar to many ICT gurus, cleared off the internet. Completely. Actually, Romeo reported, the information had been on the web until a few weeks before. And then, it disappeared without trace. This had prompted

Joe to ask for another round of chat. Which was granted. How could anyone clear information from the internet like that? To Romeo, this was unthinkable, as at least some sites were well protected. But it happened. Then Romeo reasoned through the chat that anything could actually materialize from the Chinese end of the globe. What had happened to the cars? Obviously, they had found their way into Nigeria, Romeo concluded blandly. And then to the question of whether anybody could be got to comment on the mystery, Joe would just have to visit the states himself, and see things that could not be transmitted through the internet. Things like the place of the crash test, the charred remains of the tested Macedat, et cetera. He needed to see them himself.

So the reporter was going to prepare to travel immediately. Then, it occurred to him that he had a wife; and that she was pregnant; and that the pregnancy had confined her to the bed. Oh no! He was not going to make it. Maybe his editor could embark on the trip and see what he could make of whatever was available to assess.

* * *

Gabriel's host happened to be the man with the deep voice of the recent past. But he had express support for the crusade. The man excused himself and went into an inner room, where he placed a telephone call to Nsika Isaiah reporting that the enemy supposedly at large had walked into his home asking for cooperation in his bid to wreck damage to the power brokers of the Niger Delta region. Barely two minutes after the man went into the house, Gabriel realized that he was pressed, and since his previous visits to the house had made him sufficiently familiar with the place, he helped himself.

It was at the door to the toilet that he overheard his host mention his name. The man was actually in the toilet which Gabriel was about to enter. So he stopped, first surprised that his dependable friend to whom he had already said too much was actually a mole, second alarmed that he was already in trouble. And the opposition in situations like these was certain to be after life.

Gabriel took a quick decision as he stood at the entrance of the toilet. He was going to take the bastard by surprise and take his life immediately. But just then, another soul entered the house who would either witness the encounter or get killed himself in the process. Unfortunately, Gabriel knew this new comer: he was a stubborn fighter who was certain to be armed. Thus as the host stepped out of the toilet, Gabriel reported that he was far too late for a very important engagement. He must leave at once. But he was going to return immediately after the engagement. He gave the time of his expected return to be latest a day's time. That was his mistake, for then he realized that enemies would be after him in another twenty-four hours.

How far could he possibly go?

He rushed out of the place anyway, and resolved to consider his chances later.

NINE

Omuya had not been himself since the China trip. He had asked over and over again how the whole arrangement was going to be leak-proof knowing well that it would soon steer public reaction. But it had always been Chikodi answering him with a sort of ridiculously confident smile. "Everything's taken care of. Nobody can find anything to nail us. Nothing on the internet and nothing outside it. And whatever anyone even finds, we'd simply claim ignorance…and defend our brand passionately. It's a matter of image laundering. And you know that the name of the sample tested was actually Macedat, not Cemento. We're selling Cemento, not Macedat, and as a matter of fact, we have no knowledge of or contact with Macedat or its makers. It's a simple thing."

Now as expected public reaction to the cars is overwhelmingly positive. And the slogan, as preached by the adverts, had been 'cars for all', a phrase that appealed so perfectly to the materialistic side of everybody. Who could possibly scorn a good thing like mobility–or the sheer pleasure of owning a car? However, intelligence report had it that certain people had already started asking critical questions. The more frightening was the report that somebody in the US was also involved in the prying business. And in America, Omuya knew, information was not a subject of concealment. If it existed, it had to also be available somehow. Only that people may need to know where to get it.

"Let's be a little proactive on this matter. What are we going to do should the snoopy persons happen upon what we may consider damaging?" Omuya directed this question at nobody in particular; he just asked, his back toward his partners as he gazed at nothing exactly through the window.

As usual, Chikodi had an answer. "We've prepared the ground already for a fight and it will only be in our favor. Believe that. Journalists know that though unexpressed they can't take our millions and stab us in the back, ethic or no ethic. That they have taken it, they must stand by us, or at the very least remain passive keeping their findings in the drawers while only reporting fractions of whatever anybody says. We don't demand more than that, actually. Besides, by the time anything can be proven the cars would have been sold out." He said this last sentence with a tint of smile breaking on his face.

And Omuya knew that arguing would make no difference. But there was still an angle he wanted to at least bring to the attention of his partners. "Government has invested heavily into this project and is forcing, at least as it were, civil servants into it; how do we handle them should they react?"

This obviously annoyed Chikodi. "Hah! Omuya, don't tell me that you won't defend this straight forward issue before government were you called upon to do so? The same argument goes for them and the media guys. They can't deny the fact that there has to be payback on our huge financial support at election time. Or whatever support they expect from us in the future. There may be hitches, but they can't turn their back on us. In spite of the circumstances, anyway, the cars remain very good for its price. And nothing stops people from exercising care while driving. This is a non issue; let's not drag it too far. And to correct an impression, I don't thing government is forcing; government is encouraging people to take advantage of the once-in-a-lifetime opportunity by giving them incentives. That's the balanced way I see this."

At that point, Nsika's phone rang. "Yes, what's it again?"

The man on the other end sounded slightly alarmed, or so Nsika thought he sensed in his voice. He had called earlier reporting that Gabriel had resurfaced and was working with an investigator looking for evidence against sons and daughters of the Niger Delta land who were exploiting the region. And the instruction had been clear: kill him. Which was supposed to be easy since the young man was right in his home. But up till now, Omuya's worry about non-issues had delayed his raising it for discussion. But now the man had just reported that Gabriel had left. Alive.

"You must be mad!" Nsika bellowed, forgetting that he was in the company of his partners, who still had no idea of what the problem could be, only that it had to do with their business. The other people in the room, on their part were already alarmed and were now on their feet, facing him. He bellowed again, "You are mad!"

"Sir..." the man on the other end tried to say, but Nsika cut him shut.

"You are mad." He struck Omuya ferociously, instantly revealing to both Omuya and Chikodi their ignorance of their friend's violent tendencies all these years. "You mean a person meant to be killed suddenly resurfaced in your home telling you that he is now planning to destroy us, and you let him go? No, what exactly is it that you are saying?"

"It's strange...," the man tried to explain. But again, Nsika cut him shut.

"Look, you have nothing to say about this. Go after him immediately. If he's not dead before the end of this day, you may have to ..." Nsika realized the weight of what he was almost saying and stopped the sentence midway. No matter what, he had always maintained, this man could not be killed because he was his only

107

cousin. And in spite of his many blunders, the man had always been spared of the penalty for non-delivery at critical times. Thus, what Nsika realized was that it must not be heard then that he was the one now threatening his own cousin with death. He lowered the phone without saying anything further.

And without disconnecting. So, the man at the other end of the line was to hear every word of the discussion that followed. Nsika looked up at Chikodi and blurted, "Can you imagine? He called me that Gabriel had surfaced in his home and was asking for his assistance on the investigation that would ultimately zero in on us primarily, and I gave him the express instruction to execute him. Now he's reporting that the guy had gone through his fingers."

"We must have this guy himself killed tonight. He's a sellout. Omuya, call our CSO in Port Harcourt and tell him to take care of the bastard." Chikodi was undoubtedly determined to do that.

"Which guy?" Nsika wanted to know.

"I don't know. Both of them. Gabriel, and the fool who lost him."

"Do you realize…?"

"Cut that crab, Nsika. Even you have pronounced the judgment. We cannot allow him to destroy us and all that we have built simply because he's your cousin. You know that yourself."

Now Nsika knew that he was losing the battle for his cousin's life. And he could no longer push. He then resorted to tactical pleading. "But I think we should give him some time–I mean till the end of the day to execute this project."

"That," Chikodi asserted, "will not make him live; note that. We've had enough of this mess. We've already given him years. We can't give him forever. And if he succeeds now, it does not absorb him of the fact that he is becoming our Achilles' heel. With him around, we're too exposed. And we can't just sack him like they do in the civil service. No. this is clearly overdue. Forget sentiment."

Nsika himself knew that it was overdue. So he gave up and said something rather unthinkable in his situation, "So who takes over there?"

That question was, actually, the turning point for the man listening in on the exchange. The man clenched his teeth and fist at the same time. It never occurred to him that he was walking at the precipice; and now, he had just got the inkling, nay, fact that death was at the door, too close. The thought made him sick.

Very sick.

Now he must partner with Gabriel if he ever was going to live. But he had no idea where to find him. All that was clear at the moment was that he did not even have the liberty to enter his room as close as it was, to pick anything, not money, not change of clothing. Nothing. He must run for his life.

But, to where?

He had absolutely no idea where to turn, for the safest place might actually be the heart of the enemy's territory, just like his home was to Gabriel a few minutes ago. He left through the rear door. Oh! He has also forgotten to take any weapon. He must not return. And it was that last precaution that saved his life, for the man with the mandate to execute him stepped into the house through the front door the same second.

TEN

Joseph Meals hated situations like this. Just at the time he needed speed and concentration, his wife's pregnancy got unexpectedly complicated, and she had to just put up in the hospital till the day of delivery. Joseph looked squarely at the doctor as they both stepped out of Joyce's ward, "But you promised that this would not relapse. You were sure, doctor." This sounded very much like accusation, but Joe did not care at the moment. He was getting frustrated. "What happened? Why the sudden change?"

The doctor on his part was very calm. "You see, Mr. Meals, this happens often. You have to trust our judgment." He repositioned his glasses. "When we assured you that there was not likely to be further complication, we were not absolute; what we said was that if she would avoid stress completely, and try and have enough rest actually. We made it clear that her condition required that she remain in bed almost all through this period. Now you'll be the one to help us here; did she comply?"

Joseph was not instant in answering. "Yes. She only stepped out of the house...I...think once or twice within the last week, and maybe she went to the kitchen once in a while. She's not doing anything hard; I can tell you that doctor."

The doctor's voice was suddenly musical. "You see, Mr. Meals, even walking to the kitchen is hard labor in her condition; we made that clear. Anyway, we need not argue over this. She'll be okay here."

This, again, infuriated Joseph, as he had always suspected owners of private hospitals of admitting patients unnecessarily all because of what they were going to charge for their bed. But he kept himself under control this time. "How long will this take?" he inquired.

"We really can't tell now, Mr. Meals." Then the doctor felt he picked something troubling in Joe's look. "Or is there anything wrong?"

"Many," Joseph confessed. "I'm very busy on a work at the moment, and shuttling between work and home has been difficult enough. Now this."

The doctor was sympathetic, and actually appeared to give it a thought for a while. His answer, anyway, could well have been given without any consideration. It was routine. "But, if you don't mind, we have services that cover her welfare. We could even give her a dedicated nurse to tend to her round the clock. As long as she's here, of course she eats here. I mean if you can afford it, her staying here will even be less stressful for you." A faint smile appeared on the doctor's lips. "All you need to concern yourself with is flowers and the likes each time you visit. That's all."

Joseph's first instinct was that Joyce would not take it. But he did not say it. He would have to just convince her, for that, borne out of selfishness or not, appeared to be the best option at the moment.

* * *

Another enemy at large! Chikodi looked Nsika straight in the eye and accused him of being a party to the mess. And of probably nursing an ulterior motive. Nothing that Nsika said made any sense. Not even to Omuya, who appeared quiet through the hot exchange. He cursed the 'stupid' boy, as he now regarded his own cousin, but it would not make any difference. He had just pleaded on behalf of the boy, and the boy had disappeared. There was absolutely nothing he could do to defend himself now. Only to ensure the boy was found. He personally spoke with the agent at Port Harcourt promising him personal reward if he could deliver the boy dead or alive before the end of the day.

Before the end of the day!

All through the process Omuya just stared at the street outside through the window. Of course he was turning something around in his mind. But whatever it was he did not appear ready to share with anyone. In the street, he observed, people were just going about their normal lives without fear of anything. Though many of them were poor, they were still surviving. A teenage boy hailed a taxi and jumped into the back seat pompously. An elderly woman hawked sugarcane. Somebody looking very much like a retired professor rode by on a bicycle. A middle-aged woman swept the street. In their different states, people just appeared happy and peaceful.

And here was Doctor Omuya, certain that the center could no longer hold. Yes he was sure that the roof was carving in. He suddenly whirled round and faced Chikodi.

"So," he asked extremely calmly, "where do we go from here?" Chikodi appeared to be blank, so he ventured further, "I mean enough of trading blames. There are cars to sell, there are bank issues to settle, there is the case of this desperate investigator on our heels; the absconded fellow is only one of our troubles. And since we already got somebody after him, let's trust that he won't go far and face other issues." He said all this with a very contradictory tone and posture, even leaning against the wall and crossing his legs, as if it was an issue as trivial as the infidelity of a polygamous man. Having said it, he returned to his original seat and sat down, waiting for somebody to respond.

Rather than reply, Chikodi just looked at him with

incredulity. That gave Nsika a chance to consolidate on the opportunity to change the topic. "Well," he said, "we know he can't go far." He looked at Omuya, "I think the case of this reporter is the most urgent right now. I believe that he's the one who hired the fellow in the States to ask questions around, and the fellow might as well be a private investigator, which makes him dangerous. I also believe that he's behind the scenarios at China, and is now set to make contact with us, with the confidence of someone who knows what he should not know. I think this is clear enough; we have to silence him." He said this with finality in his voice.

"But," Chikodi cut in, obviously coming to terms with this other reality, "the only person who can handle that is the one we've engaged in Port Harcourt. At least the only one that is dependable. And we won't want to use an outsider. Let's offer him some gratification and have him look away. At least until our man comes to take care of him before he changes his mind."

This seemed to have offended Omuya. "But, Chikodi, we all know that this guy will be the last to take that; he works in Joseph Meals' media house, National Trumpet, the same magazine that finished our late president. If it were possible Mr. President would have chosen that way out of ridicule. He had more money. He had the influence and even the authority. If he did not succeed with this guy...this magazine, I don't think we should even consider that option at all."

But Chikodi was sure of what he had said. "Look, this guy is of this country; if you offer him enough, his resistance will collapse. We're talking money here. Offer him in dollars, for effect, and let it go with relatively coated threats. He's no fool. He'll take it. And that will also give us time to deal adequately with him. Besides, he uses and actually believes so very much in our banks. So the amount does not really matter, we'll make it so big, possibly too big, since he will never get to reach it in his life time.

"And by the way," Chikodi now remembered, "I think I heard he was even sacked from a first-generation bank on grounds of financial impropriety. It was after then that he went into the media as a formidable business, especially banking and finance, reporter. I don't know the details, but I've heard it before. He's vulnerable. Let's offer him the bait." There was finality in his voice, the kind he used to stifle debates.

Well, if that was the case, Omuya concurred, it could be tried.

With that, contact was made with the editor in question. He answered his call on the first ring. He was surprised to learn that those he was pursuing had just decided to come to him. But he hid his excitement. He wanted an interview; they were ready to grant one, even conduct him round the warehouse where the new Cemento cars were. The editor consented before thinking of consulting with Meals.

Meals could see trouble where this editor saw an opened door, disaster where the other man saw a smooth road to success. And the man was too excited to even use his head. So Joseph wielded his authority. He was not going to honor the appointment. And he was not going to even tell them so; let them wait endlessly. It was part of the payment for their wrongs.

"It's just going to be an interview," the editor protested.

"But it's deeper than the sea," Joseph insisted.

Thus, the man left in utter disappointment. On the way, the car dealers telephoned him. There was an urgent need to meet. Plans had changed and the person to grant him the interview was going to be out of the country shortly; so if he did not come over at once, he

114

may miss the opportunity. And so the editor changed the course of his car and steered toward the beckoning opportunity.

He did conduct the interview; it was afterward that the temptation came: seventy-five thousand dollars for silence!

This was conflict between ethos and riches, loyalty and opportunity. He would need to think about it. But even then, the cheque of the first part of the payment was thrust upon him. Of course he was very free to return it if he decided later that he was not interested. But there were promises of even better years ahead if he accepted it.

Thus, the car dealers stuffed seasoned dung into the editor's mouth. At home a message was already waiting for him. His bankers had transferred twenty-five thousand dollars into his account. When he did not contact the car sellers by dusk, their corporate relations manager called at his home early the following morning.

It was actually a courtesy visit. But would he be available for a birthday dinner later in the day? It was not going to take too long. Before he could say a word, an invitation card had been pushed into his hand. Well it was an innocent thing.

The party turned out to be a sort of meeting in a remote home. There it was made clear that he was now a part of the car dealership business; and it was going to be sacrilegious for him to bite the finger that fed him. Rather he would be required to supply information about the on-going inquiry that his magazine was conducting into the car sale affair.

That was not possible, he protested.

That was a small thing, the dealers pointed out. He was part of the investigation, so he need not even ask anybody anything. And nobody also needed to know that he was involved with anything other than the business of reporting. Behind this point was the threat of possible exposure of his romance with this group he was presently with.

No, the most critical pieces of information were actually far from his reach.

Exactly, the dealers said. Where were they? He should just mention it and leave them to handle the rest. He thought of this for a while. It was going to be disastrous for Joseph, and he did not want that to happen. He refused.

Then came plain threat. Faced with a gun that was put out of safety right in his presence, the editor simply explained that there was no way he was going to ask his boss for such information. And that was all the car dealers needed. They let the editor go, having ensured that he was going to die in an auto crash in a few minutes.

Miles before he drove into the busy streets of Lagos, armed robbers waylaid him and took away his laptop, camera, money, and, of course, life. Then they put his corpse in the driver's seat and pushed the car into a canal.

Joseph did not know which was more devastating: the death of his right hand man, the editor of his magazine, or the inferno at his publishing house. He knew not what to do or where to go or whom to call. He just paced the length and breadth of his garage. Then somebody from the hospital called apologizing profusely for disturbing. But the hospital would need his consent as regarding his wife's condition.

Rather than answer, Joseph just slumped onto the floor and began to sob. The ringing of the telephone interrupted him five minutes later. But he did not even answer the call. He just picked his car key and sprinted out of the house.

Joseph drove so recklessly getting to the hospital in one piece was a miracle. His wife had suddenly gone into labor, and must undergo a caesarean section.

"Please, sign here," the doctor said thrusting a pen into his hand while at the same time placing his free hand where the signature had to be.

"How is my wife?" Joseph demanded rudely. "I need to see her."

"Mr. Meals," the doctor said in an urgency–coated calm, "you cannot go into the theatre now. But I assure you she's alright. She'll be alright."

"No. I want to see my wife!" Joseph insisted stubbornly.

Then the theatre nurse who had been passive all the while lost her temper. "This man, why are you behaving like a baby? He said your wife will be alright, and you're still wasting time, what's your problem? Do you want to take the delivery yourself?" The woman charged as if she were going to slap Joseph if he attempted further protest.

Perhaps Joseph thought so, for he just reached straight for the paper and signed without even checking what he was appending his signature to.

Then the two people picked the paper and hurried out of the room, leaving him standing alone. And wondering. Right on his feet, it occurred to Joseph that he needed to see the chubby pastor again. The void was still there, and the present complications were too much for him. He needed help. In the mean time, he sank into the upholstery in the doctor's room and began to direct some incoherent words to God in the name of prayer.

***

So far, Gabriel had made some progress. He had got the testimony of a few people, and hoped to get some more. The only difficulty he saw ahead now was how to get at least one militant who would testify convincingly. And to worsen that, he had become a wanted man in the world of the militants.

He had to tread carefully. But he must get a militant, especially one already at his wit's end. Because that was exactly the frame of mind that was necessary for success in this assignment. He thought he had almost got it: a guy who had been betrayed many times by his own compatriots and had lost the courage to continue in the struggle for freedom. The man had once told Gabriel that betrayals would always frustrate every good effort and it was at the verge of success that the blow would always be delivered. At the time, no word of Gabriel's had been able to rekindle his interest. Now Gabriel hoped the man would believe in this approach and lend his voice to this other way to freedom.

Now Gabriel was already in the neighborhood. But in order to get to his destination under the cover of the night, he drove into a back street and parked. Then he ambled into a beer parlor, where he was going to mark the next four hours. He selected a seat facing the main entrance of the beer parlor. He could also see through the door, the road outside. The windows to both sides of the door were wide open such that he could see almost 50 meters of the road outside clearly. As he drank, Gabriel took his time to observe the street, the passersby, the cars, the houses, et cetera; for there was nothing else he could think of doing.

Outside, nymphets were beginning to parade the street in their bid to attract boys. Gabriel could tell that they were only doing it for the fun of it. He wondered whether they were not going to get more than the fun they sought by the appearance of the boys paying attention. On the other side of the road, men were gathering under a tree to play draft and *ayo*. Gabriel noticed that each arrival did so with boastful noise. Here, everyone claimed to be the best.

Then the car passed again. How had he ever missed it before? For one, the car looked too good for this neighborhood. Then, it moved too slowly for sheer pleasure and had already passed more than six times. This time, Gabriel focused on it. He needed to see who was behind the wheel, and who else was inside along with the driver. He wanted to guess the person's intention by whatever he was able to see. He looked very closely.

It was bad news.

Really bad news. One that made him think he was not likely to be alive to conclude this enquiry. Well, the laptop he carried had an express access to the internet. He quickly launched onto the web and forwarded all that he had got to Joseph Meals. He added a note that he was in danger, and might not make it. But he was going to try his best. Then he expressed his hope that what had already been got would at least amount to something.

He simply closed the lid of the computer and went to take a seat right outside the beer parlor. With the pattern already established, he expected to see the car again. And then to do something about the man behind the wheel. Though what he was going to do he was yet to decide. But this was the operations partner of the man he trusted so much that he revealed all his mission to, who immediately turned round to relay his secret to the very enemies of the mission. He could have no other assignment here now than to kill. Gabriel was sure of that.

Indeed, the car came by again and the man behind the wheel also surveyed the environment. Gabriel even thought the man saw him. From the look of things, they might have locked gazes for about a split second.

Unless the man did not recognize him. But he would be a fool not to.

However, whatever doubt remained within Gabriel flew when he saw the man pull up the car at the shoulder of the road just about 120 meters down the road.

Thus, Gabriel now excused himself and went into the toilet. Maybe luck was going to favour him. It was a rule that at times like this; an exposed militant fearing capture should go first into the toilet from where he was to make contact with the nearest associates. If this enemy still held the false impression that Gabriel would not suspect him, he could check for him inside the toilet. Gabriel prayed he did.

And he did. As the man approached, he called out to Gabriel in a coded language, saying that he now had exactly what was needed and that it was necessary that he deliver immediately. Joseph held his peace.

At the door of the toilet, the man spoke another coded language. Gabriel held his breath.

Then the man pushed the door open, and hesitated. Gabriel raised his knife. The fool was sure to come in.

And he did. The knife pierced his neck the very instant he stuck it out to see if there was anybody inside. Gabriel then took the key from behind the door and locked as he went out. By that, it was going to be at least thirty minutes before they would discover the body.

Though it was not yet time for him to go where he intended, he decided to go immediately because he had not much time around anymore.

The welcome he got could not be placed at all. It was that of joy at seeing a fellow thought to have been dead, and that of suspicion of whether the person could actually be a ghost. Joy dominated when the man realized eventually that it was not a ghost. Gabriel only briefed his host saying that when the storm was over, he was going to give him the full story. Right now there was the need for the man to add his voice to the campaign against deprivation in the Niger-Delta region as well as give information regarding the operations of the big wigs concerned.

That the battle that has been on for many years, which had been fought with all weapons imaginable, could be won by just recoding somebody's voice was too incredulous for the man. No, the man was not going to have anything to do with another fruitless attempt. It took outright pleading to convince him, to, at least, add his voice and stay back and watch. By that, he would have nothing to lose.

If that be the case, the man revealed what he knew and supplied a hypothesis which he thought Gabriel could try. It could lead him, and whoever he was working with, to the whole truth of the Niger-Delta woes. As soon as Gabriel realized that the man had said all that he was ready to say, he rose to his feet, thanked him profusely, and promised to return when the victory was won. To that, the man only replied with a scornful nod.

And then Gabriel was gone.

When he had traveled 200 kilometers away from the village of his last crime, he pulled up at the shoulder of the road and mailed the latest piece of information to Joseph. He noted that there was not a single reply yet from Joseph, which was quite unusual. But there was nothing he could do about it on the road. So he logged out of the internet, closed the lid of his computer, and continued his journey.

ELEVEN

Yet again, Joseph's mobile phone alerted him of an e-mail. But his mind did not even go that direction. He ignored the phone and continued his wait for the door of the theatre to open and his wife wheeled out alive. The door did open eventually, but it was only the doctor who came out of the theatre and approached him with an expression that could not be read.

"Well, Mr. Meals," he said, seemingly feigning the smile he carried.

It appeared that Joseph did not hear that. "Doctor; how about my wife?" he wanted to know.

"Your wife made it," the doctor informed him, moving rapidly toward his office. Joseph crossed his path and he simply told him to step into the office where they could talk. In the office, the doctor expressed his regret about the baby. According to him, the baby struggled for too long before the caesarean section could be carried out. So it was actually brought out dead.

Joseph's head dropped in sorrow. In his bid to encourage him, the doctor placed his hand on his shoulder and said, "Mr. Meals, the good news is that nothing happened to your wife's womb. So, there's a very bright hope for her. And you've now learnt how to ensure that your next doesn't suffer similar fate."

Joseph quietly removed the doctor's hand. "It's my fault. Dr., I killed that baby. If my wife should ever get to know that I delayed, she'd never forgive me." He looked the doctor straight in the eye now. "And you see, again, it's not my fault. My life got complicated just as you called. And now I've lost a second in less than three hours."

The doctor just looked at him, having not the

faintest idea of what he was talking about.

"So, when do I collect my wife?"

"Mr. Meals?" the doctor was a little alarmed.

"Yes," Joseph answered, suddenly getting alarmed himself.

"Please try and compose yourself. There are still many babies to be brought into this world by that woman; I can tell you that. Don't allow this to weigh you down."

"I know. Thank you, doctor." Joseph sank into a seat and immediately began to check his mails: two from Gabriel, one from Murphy, three from Romeo. He figured that what Gabriel had got from the Niger-Delta was sufficient, especially since he himself was going to be the principal testifier. And his testimony alone was satisfactorily revealing. Joseph mailed him back warning against taking any risk whatsoever. He should just find his way back to Lagos and finish up what had been started. Murphy by mysterious means passed across to Joseph the information that security needed to be beefed up around his home and office. And his editor's precedence of possible financial impropriety was enough to engender suspicion. While Joe knew that that was vital information, he noted that it came a little too late. The worst had already happened. But what scared Joseph in the mail was the point that the enemies were closing in on him already because his investigation of the car deal had generated strife within government functionaries. He had to now work underground, and, very importantly keep his data offshore, because theft or destruction of his equipment was imminent.

That made sense to Joseph because there had already been a fire at his office, only that whoever did it acted on incomplete information. So Joseph Meals put all his findings in one folder and mailed to Romeo in the US. He actually did that before opening Romeo's mail. There was now a link between the Macedat and the Cemento. They were one. Proofs also emerged from China that consolidated their being one and the same. Testimony of the wife of a staff of the company who died while testing one of the cars had been got. And since the poor widow was not in the US where the car makers thought she had been properly hid, she could be reached anytime. Pictures and copies of technical assessment of the car brand were also included in the mail.

Thus, Joseph sent another mail that he would prefer to transfer to the United States to put the story together since he was no longer safe in Nigeria. Would Romeo be kind enough to host him? As an afterthought, he included that his wife just had a still birth. As he clicked on send, he remembered that he was still in the hospital. As a matter of fact, it was then that he noticed that the doctor had been sitting beside him, confused.

"Doctor?" he asked.

"Yes, Mr. Meals. You don't have to do this to yourself. Your wife is alright. She had been transferred to the ICU. You can see her now if you don't mind."

Joseph did not seem to assimilate what the doctor had said. "Can she be transferred to a foreign hospital, immediately?"

"Why, Mr. Meals? There's absolutely nothing wrong with her. Why would you do that?" the doctor was amazed.

"I mean I need it done immediately. Like this evening." Joseph still appeared irrational.

When all efforts of the doctor's were fruitless, he conceded and started the arrangement for the transfer of the woman to the US. They got a hospital to take her and her ticket was ready in a few hours. As a principle Joseph always went about with his international passport, which incidentally had a valid US visa. Luckily, Joyce's passport was her preferred means of identification, so it was also in the handbag right beside her. And she also had a valid visa since she was meant to travel toward the EDD of her baby and put to bed in the US.

Since the investigation was the main concern, Joseph did not bother to return home for anything. If he had done, he would have been caught by the intruder that ransacked the home for every available document relating to his bold investigation. The intruder also had the instruction to kill.

***

"Everybody has disappeared!" Chikodi said in astonishment. With the fool of Port Harcourt still at large and the man detailed to kill him found dead in a restaurant's toilet, Chikodi had lost his confidence. Things, it appeared, were no longer obeying his charge. "Friend, it will be to the good of this group to produce that fool who has already caused all this trouble at once."

Nsika rose up at once. "Are you accusing me?" he stepped forward toward Chikodi, "Are you saying that I'm behind this confusion, Chikodi?"

"I'm not. I'm only making a request. But I believe only you know how to solve this without stress. Only you can tell how and where to find the betrayer." Chikodi now stepped toward him, standing right in front of him. "And I am saying if you have been honest all along, we would not have got into this rut." His voice was now high and firm.

"Oh, cut that crab, Chikodi," Nsika was now fuming, restraining himself from throwing the first punch with great effort. "Cut it…"

A call reached Chikodi and when he checked the identity of the caller, he relaxed and answered it. It was the minister of transportation who was calling to inform them that the Senate had summoned him to give account of why and how his ministry had awarded a contract worth billions of Naira without due process, and had allegedly paid up even long before taking delivery of samples of the products.

"Are they out of their senses?" was Chikodi's first reaction. "Tell the Chairman of the Senate committee on transport to kill that idea immediately," he ordered and hung up the phone.

The phone rang almost immediately, and the minister insisted that the Chairman had already been contacted and he said his hands were tied. He further informed Chikodi that the bank account to which the money had been paid had already been frozen, and since the financial and economic crimes commission was involved, arrests were likely to be made within another day.

"You must be out of your mind," Chikodi bellowed. "And don't ever threaten me again in your life. Do you hear me? Is it me you want to arrest or Mr. President? Go and tell Mr. President that I said that: He should tell those guys to stop this nonsense. Tell him that, since you are close to him." Again, Chikodi hung up the phone, and faced his colleagues.

"The Senate is investigating the car sale deal. They want to make arrests. But I think I've dealt with them for now. What do we do in the short term?"

Nsika suggested that the first measure remained to locate Joseph Meals and stop him from publishing. And with the information that Gabriel might be collaborating with him, he might have already got facts that could nail many coffins.

If only the threat posed by Meals could be removed,

things could still be rescued. Then the managers of the banks had to be alerted that they had to cover the vacuum that would be left should the government withdraw the money already paid. It was the banks that would shoulder the responsibility, pending the time that issues would be sorted out.

Then there was the need to meet the President one-on-one. He had to use his influence here, regardless of what reaction it was going to rouse in the public. Were they to request to visit the state house, or invite Mr. President?

Something in between would be best. Ask Mr. President to a meeting at a location within Abuja. That meant that one of them must be on the way to Abuja immediately. Since others would have to manage the other aspects of the crisis, who would go became an issue.

It was at that point that they realized that Omuya had been quiet through the frantic moments. What was the problem with him?

Nothing.

Would he want to meet with Mr. President?

Omuya was reluctant, but he would. He had no choice anyway. And since he had been most successful with politicians whenever they had to be handled one-on-one, he knew his refusal would be a disaster.

In Abuja, Omuya handled Mr. President pretty well. The Senate President and Minister of Transportation were also present. At the end it was agreed that the contract be cancelled, and due process be followed. But Omuya was assured that it was only going to be formality; the job was for him, other bidders would only heighten the façade. And it was going to shut the mouth of the aggrieved Senators and members of the public. No mention was made of the quality of the cars. Immediately after the one-hour meeting Omuya shook

Mr. President and his entourage and returned to Lagos. Thing had started to look up again.

TWELVE

Somehow Gabriel ran into the man with the deep voice at a filling station. The size of his car's engine was helpful in his hurry to get back to Lagos and see what was going on with Joseph Meals. He overtook every vehicle he had met on the way without fuss. Then one, a Mercedes had been difficult first because the road was not so wide and also because the man himself was going at top speed. Once Gabriel attempted to overtake him, but when he was right beside him, he had spotted another car coming ahead. So he had fallen back behind the car. But before falling back he had tried to see who it was that was driving that fast on the narrow lane. That speed, Gabriel had considered, was for the desperate like him.

It was then that he saw the man; the man with the deep voice. The man obviously did not see him because just then he saw a ditch ahead and concentrated on getting over it. With this development, Gabriel just relaxed behind the Mercedes, now debating as he drove how he was going deal with the man without getting into trouble. And then the man had turned into a filling station at the outskirt of a small town, and a short while later, Gabriel had also turned in, parking directly behind him.

Because it was Gabriel who came and parked behind the man, he had had the surprise weapon. And because it was not going to be nice killing at the station, Gabriel had touched the man's waist with the barrel of his well concealed pistol and ordered him into the Maxima. He knew the man's mission, he assured him, and was going to turn the table. In the car, Gabriel stripped the man of all his weapons and then tied him hand and feet and threatened to kill at the slightest sign of struggle. Then Gabriel drove the man into a narrow farm road, and found a secluded location. He then parked the car at the middle of the road and began his interrogation earnestly.

The confession was too nauseating for Gabriel. The man started with a confession that he was also a victim of the process: that it was not his fault at all. As Gabriel's predecessor in their Movement, he had been vibrant, firing on all cylinders, actually until this group of men in suits intruded into his world. They convinced him to work with certain men who were going to be so helpful to the crusade and him personally. It had been a good offer, and he had taken it, only to find that he was meant to do what was contrary to his mission. But they had already done so many things in his name so much so that the revelation of only one of those incriminating deeds to the other militants would have lead to his outright rejection and eventual death.

That was when he realized that he had been stuck with this group of criminals. They had made it clear that they needed someone who was familiar with and actually acceptable by the people of the Niger Delta Region to act as their link person. It was this person who would be contacting the militants, helping them, especially in ways that would encourage violence, and will also be in touch with the oil companies as peacemaker. In short, they needed a fronting person, and as an ex-militant this man with the deep voice had been the choice. He had been compelled. Then, the man had confessed of his role as the mastermind of Gabriel's setup, of his assignment to execute him when he, Gabriel, had shown up at his home at the wrong time. But somehow Gabriel had escaped, and that had lead to his discovering that even if he succeeded in killing Gabriel, somebody must have been after him by now. And it was not going to take long before he himself was killed. So, when he saw in his mirror that the person in the car behind him was Gabriel he had been happy, because his intention had been of peace. Then he had driven into the station to create room for a meeting where they were going to talk. He had not known that Gabriel had somehow discovered the instruction to execute him, thus had not prepared for any form of violence. Only for Gabriel to spring a surprise.

Now, why not go into partnership to see what they could do with their common enemy?

The man with the deep voice had noted that he was not quite afraid of death, but that it was going to be a fatal mistake for Gabriel to kill him since he was not going to be able to fight alone: Gabriel alone could not win this battle. He certainly needed the collaboration of somebody who had partnered with these criminals.

Since the men in suit had approached Gabriel too, he believed this confession, at least to a large extent. Gabriel recorded it. He had also taken the man's photograph during the confession. He immediately uploaded the data and mailed to Joseph Meals. He then added that should Joseph be interested in interviewing the man himself, he was going to hold him captive for some time. Then Gabriel put the man in shackles again and resumed the journey toward Lagos. "If you're ever going to live," Gabriel emphasized, "You're going to have to partner with me until this siege is over. I mean, if I discover that you've lied, you're dead. "

***

In spite of his success in business, Chikodi had no child. And his marriage had been thirteen years. Unfortunately, he was Igbo, a tribe that measures a woman's productivity by the number of children she bears. As a matter of fact Chikodi's mother's way of describing the situation was that he had married a he goat. But this would be about to change. Immediately his wife left the hospital with the news of her pregnancy, the doctor called him. So, he had even started preparing for the celebration before the woman's arrival. He watched from the window as she jumped out of the car and flew up the stairs. "Honey!" she exclaimed from the staircase, "I'm pregnant!"

"Are you serious!" he exclaimed rather than ask. Then he met her with a big hug. Just then Omuya stepped into the sitting room, gun in hand, locking the door behind him.

"To go straight to the point," he said promptly, "I'm here for war."

From the look on the man's face Chikodi knew he meant what he had said. Then he began to plead. That took up to five minutes, but it still did not save his life.

When Omuya was done he said emotionlessly to the man's wife, "you won't understand, my dear. But if you don't mind, I can still tell you the story. Or better still, I'll put it in writing and pass it to you when you are through the most critical state of losing your husband." He then took the woman by the hand and led her to the bathroom where he tied her hands, feet, and mouth. "Don't worry; people will find you at the appropriate time," he assured her, and then disappeared through a security door that only Chikodi supposedly knew about.

Nsika's home was not far away, a reality that had been deliberately executed for the smooth running of their business empire. But for the sake of time, Omuya still went in his car. He had to be true to his promise that he needed to get the whole job done quickly. He approached the house through a back street and went a few yards past it before pulling up at the shoulder of the street. He picked his knife and pistol and went straight for a secret door very few knew existed. As he went through the door he thought within himself, with their own hands the wicked always chart the course of their nemesis. Nsika's wife happened to be the extreme opposite of being barren– she was a baby-machine, having produced five, a set of twins and a set of triplets, in four years. So the house was going to be a private crèche. But the crowds were not going to even know a thing about this. They were just going to find out later. It was meant to be a mystery. Omuya paused behind the door leading to the study. As a rule, the study was out of bound to all. And they all knew better than break that rule. Nsika could be mean.

When he had ascertained that there was nobody in the study, he stepped inside and shut the door behind him. He then went to create a comfortable place for himself behind a bookshelf. The next line of action was to call the target into the study somehow. And looking at the items on the work desk, he already knew how. He called the number meant to be used to reach Nsika only on emergency. The phone was right there on the desk, and must ring aloud so the target must rush in to answer the call.

Indeed, he rushed in.

Omuya stepped into the open just then and started by locking the door. Then he trailed the gun on Nsika's heart. "You see," he said calmly, "I'm here to take your life." As he said this, the man's hands went up in the air in plea. Omuya on his part continued to advance toward him, the gun still pointed, and the other hand behind him.

"No you can't do this at this time Omuya. We're just at the verge of owning the world. No…"

"Precisely," Omuya cut in, "We're pushing hard to own the world without regard for what becomes of others. Or without regards to what happens to the world itself. We're going to own the world so we can destroy it. Indeed we want to own the world. But of what use will the world itself be afterward?" He paused, not really expecting any answer. "Your vision makes me sick. If you've got an eye you should have known since. Anyway, that will soon be story. The reporter escaped, and is now ready to publish his findings. He got what he wanted, facts you'd never believe anyone could. And they were accurate. I mean facts that makes useless every veil on those corporations, and oil bunkering deals, the computer scams and banking paper works, and of course, the Cemento." Omuya appeared to smile briefly. "By the way, I'm already wasting time here." He took the final step, and with the hand that had been behind him produced the knife and stabbed Nsika in the neck. He knocked him over with the butt of the gun, and placed him gently against the wall.

Omuya retreated through the way he had come.

***

Joseph Meals was rounding off his report on the car deal when the mail got into his box. "I've no way of reaching you by phone, but we need to talk. I assure you it will make your report richer and absolutely convincing. True. For instance, the main actors in what has become the bad news about Nigeria are now dead. You will soon hear about that. But very important, if you delay in calling me, you may never get to the root of the matter, because the only source you can ever get may not have too long to live anymore." The author gave a Nigerian telephone number and promised to be expecting the call. It was important that Joseph be fast about it.

Since it was a Nigerian number and Joe was far away, he felt no restraint to making the call.

The confession was raw. Unfortunately, Joe had no means of recording it. But just then, the man offered to send details by mail. And of course, he challenged Joe to ask around, especially in political circles about Omuya. He gave names of corporations under which the group operated, and promised to also send their registration papers. He spoke of the chip inbuilt into the computers sold to Aso Rock, National Assembly and all the offices at the Federal Secretariat, with which affairs of government were monitored. They were verifiable. Then he provided the missing link between these men and the restiveness in the Niger Delta region.

Immediately after Joseph hung up, he called the only politician he recognized as his own associate. Nura knew those men alright. They were even the key sponsors of the party in the last general elections. He also knew that a particular company supplied computers to the federal secretariat and others. But he did not know who owned the company. He also did not know the mysterious link between the men and the Niger Delta. Or did not count it believable.

Murphy may know, Joe reasoned. So he called the prison, and had the prisoner taken to the comfort of the Warden's office for the call. It was no secret, so, the Warder could stay if he so wished. The telephone conversation turned out to be very brief. With the help of his old prison pal, Murphy had already compiled the facts and was praying for an opportunity to test it. He was beginning to lose hope when he did not hear from Gabriel after his escape and news of Joe's lost baby got through. But now, he simply confirmed Joseph's proposition, and so the call ended. That was exactly the theory he and his friend here in the prison believed. They had been proven right. Joseph should just go ahead; it was another breakthrough.

By this time, the news of the two dead men was already out. But details were scanty. One was murdered, but the other appeared to have committed suicide. They were rich. They were friends, and probably business partners. And that was all. All there could have been, actually. Except that, the suspected killer of the murdered one was allegedly his close associate.

Joseph knew that no investigation could possibly reveal more than that. The connections were just too deep and well concealed. Joseph even suspected that the associate in question was the very one that spoke with him on the phone, though the reason for his breakdown, would, at the very least, be unthinkable. But Joe believed that he was the one.

Somehow Gabriel has also been able to send a more revealing piece, this time, accompanied by photographs. The piece had completely demystified the Niger Delta connection. As he relished this point, yet another set of documents arrived in his mailbox and confirmed his suspicion of the last caller being a member of the criminal group.

THIRTEEN

Following the testimony of Chikodi's widow, the police arrested Omuya. When he was interrogated, he neither pleaded guilty nor denied committing the crime. He just kept quiet and appeared extremely peaceful. He knew his trial was going to be a high-profile one, which would afford him a platform to say in public how he had come to live this way. It was not going to get him justified, but at least it would further open the eyes of the world to the lure of corruption. Maybe then the powers that be would summon the courage to sort it all out. All that he said, at the moment, was that he was a medical doctor who set out to save lives, but got pushed to the wall.

***

REVEALED: THE MASTERMINDS OF THE NATION'S WOES. That was the title of NATIONAL TRUMPET magazine's cover story. It provided details of atrocities perpetrated by the trio, as well as how highly placed government officials became indebted to them. With the magazine already on sale, Joseph felt as if a heavy load had been lifted off his shoulder. Now he could afford nine hours of sleep. By the time he woke up, the power pack of his laptop had disappeared. When he asked Joyce, she merely stated that the child that works hard must equally make out time for relaxation. "By the way," she added. "I got us tickets to the quarter finals of the tennis tournament going on in town." She flashed a mischievous smile. "The game is at six tomorrow evening. For today, I got us DVDs of three new movies and some musicals." Then she added as if it was something trivial, that she had Romeo lock them in and go with the key until evening.

"Well, fine," Joseph resigned. "Maybe we should arrange to visit a beach and a park also." He poured two cups of tea and handed one to Joyce. "At least we now know there is yet another little light shining from a corner of the darkness hovering over our nation." He planted a kiss on her nose, "So which movie do we begin with?"

[THE END]